Carol handed Anne a thin file. "There hasn't been an inquest yet, but a guy called Ian Stewart apparently killed himself. It's Wally Ford's case, but I've taken it out of his hands for the moment. I want you to look through the file, make a few phone calls, then give me your assessment."

"You don't think it's suicide?"

"It's probably what it appears to be, but there may be a connection to another death. I'm not saying any more, Anne. I want your unbiased opinion."

"And what if there is something suspicious?"

Carol grinned. "Then things will get interesting, fast."

Visit

Bella Books

at

BellaBooks.com

or call our toll-free number

1-800-729-4992

BLOOD LINK

THE 15th DETECTIVE INSPECTOR
CAROL ASHTON MYSTERY

BY
CLAIRE McNAB

Bella
BOOKS

2003

Bella Books, Inc.
P.O. Box 10543
Tallahassee, FL 32302

Printed in the United States of America on acid-free paper
First Edition

Editor: Greg Herren
Cover designer: Bonnie Liss (Phoenix Graphics)

ISBN 1-931513-27-9

For Sheila

ACKNOWLEDGMENTS

Many thanks to my editor Greg Herren; proofreader Judy Eda; and typesetter Therese Szymanski.

ABOUT THE AUTHOR

CLAIRE MCNAB is the author of fourteen Detective Inspector Carol Ashton mysteries: *Lessons in Murder, Fatal Reunion, Death Down Under, Cop Out, Dead Certain, Body Guard, Double Bluff, Inner Circle, Chain Letter, Past Due, Set Up, Under Suspicion, Death Club,* and *Accidental Murder.* She has written two romances, *Under the Southern Cross* and *Silent Heart,* and has co-authored a self-help book, *The Loving Lesbian,* with Sharon Gedan. She is the author of four Denise Cleever thrillers, *Murder Undercover, Death Understood, Out of Sight,* and *Recognition Factor.*

CHAPTER ONE

"Looks like a simple accident, Carol," said Mark Bourke. "Several witnesses, one close by who saw the whole thing, so no suggestion of anything else. The local cop shop should have dealt with it. We wouldn't be here if she didn't have a famous dad."

Clad in tight black jeans and a scarlet shirt darkened by blood, the woman was sprawled face-down near the rear of a fire-red Lamborghini with its boot open. She still wore one high-heeled shoe. The other was lying on its side two meters away. Keys were clenched in the bloodied fingers of her left hand, on the back of which was a small tattoo of a black rose. Brand-name shopping bags lay scattered. One had burst, revealing the lustrous green fabric of

1

some item of clothing. A handbag had spilled most of its contents on the ground—a wallet, gold compact, a Palm with an embossed, custom-made cover, a silver pen.

Skewed at an angle, its driver's door open, a shabby light truck sat twenty meters away, guarded by a patrol officer. Dark skid marks showed where the driver had violently braked. Broken headlight glass glittered fitfully as the sun broke through.

Carol stood back to survey the larger scene. The sky was full of racing, tattered clouds. The bland beige buildings of the shopping mall sat in a sea of parked cars. A chill wind fluttered the crime-scene tape enclosing the section of the parking area in which they stood. Squad cars sat at each end of this section, preventing entry or exit of vehicles. Shoppers denied access to their cars had bunched together under the wary gaze of another officer, who was noting down their names. Others, drawn by the drama promised by police activity and the presence of an ambulance, lingered on their way to and from the shopping center.

"Set up screens," said Carol, noting the first of the TV vans pulling into the parking area. "The least we can do is give her some privacy—" She broke off at the mosquito buzz of an approaching helicopter. "Well, there goes that thought, Mark. This is shaping up to be your well-known media frenzy."

"Inspector Ashton?" A uniformed female officer, seeming to Carol about eighteen, approached, grave with the importance of the moment. "The number plate checks out. The Lamborghini is regis-tered to Ms. Rule."

"Martina Rule, heir to billions, dies in a parking lot of a suburban mall," said Bourke, a wry smile on his blunt-featured face. "Who'd have thought it?"

Carol's mobile phone chirped. "Carol Ashton." She listened, said, "Yes, everything indicates it's Martina Rule. Apparently she was walking to her car when she was struck by a vehicle. Death was prob-ably instantaneous." She paused, then added, "No, I haven't inter-viewed the driver yet . . . Of course, Commissioner. Thank you."

2

As she ended the call, Bourke gave a low whistle. "The Commissioner's involved?"

"He's a friend of Rule's, so he's about to speak to him personally."

Bourke made a face. "I reckon Rule already has the bad news. The patrol officers first on the scene took one look at her driving license, recognized the name, and wisely kicked the whole problem upstairs, but it was a bit late by then." He gestured at a second TV news truck entering the parking area. "See what I mean? The word's well and truly out."

Carol looked down at the broken body. Thurmond Rule's daughter had long been a staple of the gossip pages, her long, rather horsy features captured in photographs at every notable movie premiere, art show or society function. The Rule name made her a must-invite, in spite of widely reported accounts of wild behavior, plus her tendency to viciously attack perceived rivals to her social position.

Bourke supervised the placement of canvas screens to conceal the body from the avid stares of both onlookers and the lens of television cameras set up on the roofs of the media vehicles. A couple of on-air reporters, held back by the tape and the presence of the young female constable who'd given Carol the information on the Lamborghini, yelled out questions, and were ignored.

"Here's Reynolds," said Carol, observing the police doctor squeezing his considerable self from the embrace of the Mini Cooper he had recently acquired, to the amusement of everyone except himself. Close behind him was the crime-scene van.

Reynolds wheezed his way over. Beaming at Carol, he said, "And how's my favorite blonde-bombshell inspector?"

"I'm fine, Burt. And you?"

"The wife's got me on a bloody diet—lettuce leaf and celery special." He patted his rotund stomach. "Be fading away, any day now." Switching his attention to the body at their feet, he said, "Rule's profligate daughter, eh?" plunking his medical bag beside the body. He grinned at Carol's resigned expression. "Hope you

3

weren't planning to keep a lid on it. I heard Martina Rule had been in a fatal accident on the radio while driving over."

Liz Carey, her shock of gray hair in its usual disarray, ducked her stocky body under the tape. Behind her, laden with equipment, came three members of her crime-scene team. "Hurry up, Burt," she said to the police doctor. "Haven't got all day." She jerked her head at the wider world. "They're dying like flies, out there."

Liz and Reynolds grinned at each other, knowing she was being facetious. For reasons not readily apparent, the current crime rate in New South Wales was at an all-time low in almost all categories, except, oddly, shoplifting.

"The Commissioner's involved," said Bourke.

Liz Carey snorted. "Of course the Commissioner's involved. Rule's got a billion or two kicking around. His money gives him access to anyone and everyone."

Reynolds grimaced as he lowered his bulk to kneel beside the body. "Then we'd all better do this one strictly by the book."

Aggravated by his hard-done-by tone, Carol said, "I'm sure you agree, by the book, should apply to everyone, whoever they are. The victim's relatives shouldn't make a difference."

The police doctor looked up at her with a sour smile. "Oh, yes? Remember the Courtauld case? Daddy certainly threw his weight around there."

Eight months earlier, Martina Rule had been arrested after a brawl in a nightclub, not the first in which she'd been involved. This time, however, she'd been charged with assault, having ended a heated argument with another patron by smashing a unopened champagne bottle over his head. The victim, Henry Courtauld, had ended up in hospital with severe concussion. Martina had ended up in a cell, screaming police brutality and wrongful arrest.

It had appeared to be an open-and-shut prosecution, but her father had hired experts, used private investigators, and paid for the services of the very best legal brains. Doubt was cast on every shred of evidence, witnesses recanted, the testimony of police officers was impugned. In Carol's opinion, Rule's influence and money had bought his daughter an undeserved verdict of not guilty.

Bourke conferred with one of the uniformed officers while Reynolds established that the victim was, indeed, dead. The doctor compared the ambient temperature with that of the body—plunging a thermometer into the liver—certified the time of death as within the last two hours, and packed up his things while Liz Carey's technicians took charge. Photographs and measurements taken, the body was rolled over. Diamonds glinted in her ears, a thin gold necklace gleamed. The woman has sustained some damage to her face, but the slack, bloodied features were clearly recognizable. She was indubitably Martina Rule.

"Now for the driver," said Bourke. "The patrol cops gave him a breath test for alcohol. He hadn't been drinking, and his ID checks out okay. Name's Hawkins, Sid Hawkins."

Hawkins slid out of the back seat of the squad car as soon as Carol and Bourke approached. He was a thin man with greasy hair, and an angular, discontented face. He wore grimy jeans and a tight once-white T-shirt that emphasized his incipient paunch. Jerking his thumb at the constable who'd been guarding him, he said to Carol, "This guy says you're in charge." Clearly, he wasn't impressed.

"I'm Inspector Ashton, Mr. Hawkins. Would you tell us what happened?"

"What happened was she stepped out in front of me. Didn't see her til too late." He tilted his head, apparently to gauge Carol's response, then added, "An accident. Her fault, not mine." Another pause, then, "She's dead? That right?"

"I'm afraid so."

Hawkins huffed a breath. "Jesus. This would happen to me."

Bourke said, "We'll require a written statement."

"Look, other people saw it happen, you know." He swung his narrow head around. "Some guy was right there. These other cops talked to him. Dunno where they've taken him, but he can back me up." His attention back on Carol, he said, "How long's this going to take? I'm sorry, and all that, but I've got things to do."

Carol gave him a cool, official smile. "We're all very busy, Mr. Hawkins. We'll try not to keep you too long. Please tell me in as much detail as possible what happened."

"I done it umpteen times already." When Carol didn't respond, he gave an exasperated wriggle of his shoulders. "Okay," he said in a tone of elaborate patience, "I was here at the mall to get some hardware stuff. You can look, if you don't believe me—it's in the back of me truck. So I get what I come for, and go to leave. Just minding my own business, when out of nowhere this lady's right there, in front of me. Didn't have no time to brake, or anything, at least not till after."

"Did the woman step out from between parked cars?"

Hawkins frowned at Carol's question. "No idea. Told you, I didn't see her." His hands made a sharp sound as he slapped them together. "Whack! I hit her—same time I saw her." He gave a quick, satisfied nod. "Accident, pure and simple."

Raising her eyebrows at Hawkins' insouciant attitude, Carol said, "Were you upset when you realized what had happened?"

"Upset? Of course I was bloody upset. What would you expect?" Seeking solidarity, Hawkins directed a can-you-believe-this-dumb-question glance at Bourke.

Bourke inquired, "How fast were you going?"

Hawkins narrowed his eyes. "Not speeding, if that's what you're getting at. Sure, I admit I was in a bit of a hurry, but there was no one around, see, as far as I was concerned." He sighed impatiently. "I told you, the other guy saw it all. Why don't you ask him? He'll back me up. I didn't do nothing wrong."

"So you stopped as soon as you struck the victim?"

"Look, *I'm* the victim here, being treated like a crim for no reason." Hawkins put on an air of righteousness as he continued, "And no way was I a hit and run. I slam on the brakes, jump out and run over. Straightway I could see she was a goner."

6

"Have you ever seen the woman before?"

Hawkins favored Carol with an incredulous look. "You mean do I know her? Someone like that with a fancy I-tie car? Why would I?" He folded his skinny arms. "Never saw her before in me life."

A few minutes later, the principal witness to the accident, a fidgety little man in a rumpled brown suit and creased blue shirt, confirmed Sid Hawkins' story. "I was a bit along the row, going to open my car, when this man in the truck came tooling along, not fast, mind, then this woman doesn't look, but steps right out in front of him. And he hits her."

"You didn't call out a warning, Mr. Doherty?" Bourke asked.

"No time. It was over in a second." He shook his head. "Awful. Just awful."

Carol said, "What sounds did you hear, Mr. Doherty?"

He looked confused. "Sounds?"

"When the accident happened, did you notice any sounds?"

Appearing nonplussed, he stared at her. At last he said, "Like, did she scream, you mean?"

Bourke said helpfully, "The vehicle hit the victim hard enough to kill her."

"Oh, yeah. I remember. There was a sort of thump. I don't think there was a scream." His face contorted. "Christ, it was horrible. But I saw it all, and it was an accident. I want you to know that. The driver did nothing wrong."

After she had sent both Doherty and Hawkins to the nearest police station in separate patrol cars, Carol said to Bourke before he followed to supervise their statements, "What do you think, Mark?"

"I think Martina Rule died because she was careless, and didn't look." He smiled sardonically. "Pity she couldn't have been killed by someone who at least gave a ghost of a damn, but that's the way it is."

7

CHAPTER TWO

Two days later, after Carol and Bourke had made a concentrated effort to cover all aspects of the accident, the Commissioner dispatched them to Thurmond Rule's harbor- side mansion to report in person on his daughter's death. Carol went with reluctance, knowing the Commissioner had made sure Rule got copies of all the paperwork on the case. This was simply a matter of PR.

Carol's team had a backlog of cases demanding attention. This public relations exercise would take precious time both she and Bourke could put to much better use. Resigned to the fact she would have to go, Carol had pointed out that Bourke's presence wasn't necessary. The Commissioner had insisted, saying, "Thurmond Rule may want to question your sergeant."

As Bourke drove through moderate morning traffic, Carol considered how she could reallocate duties in her team. Recently the State Coroner had publicly expressed his concern that the lack of human resources in the homicide squad was leading to a number of inadequate investigations. Carol privately agreed there was some truth in his pointed comments.

The newly reformed homicide squad was suffering from serious budgetary restraints, and although there should be seven detectives on each of the squad's seven murder teams, most were short at least one officer. In Carol's case, her team had only five members, as Terry Roham had been off on sick leave after sustaining serious injuries. She'd expected his return this week. But only this morning he'd had an unexpected relapse and been readmitted to hospital. Apart from Bourke and herself, there were only three other operational members of her team—Anne Newsome, Miles Li and Maureen Oatland. Maureen Oatland was the most experienced of the three, a large woman with a penetrating voice who had spent many years in juvenile and rape squads before coming to homicide. She was in the team temporarily, filling in for Dennis Earl, who had been accepted for special training in computer crime.

Bourke broke into her thoughts with the comment, "Looks like a fortress," as he pulled up to the huge cast-iron gates of the Rule estate. Surrounded on three sides by high sandstone walls—the fourth side was a minuscule private harbor beach—Rule's domain had two bouncer-size men guarding the entrance. Both wore extraordinarily well-tailored gray uniforms and forbidding expressions. Carol and Bourke's credentials were thoroughly checked, then they were directed to park the car just inside the wall and walk the rest of the way on a driveway that curved out of sight over a slight rise.

"Have to hand you off to the next post," rasped the larger of the two men. His companion spoke into a phone, apparently alerting the next ring of security they were on their way. He walked close behind them until a neat guard house came into view, then halted to make sure they reached it before turning and retracing his steps.

"Too much money has too many strings attached," Bourke remarked to Carol as the second two-guard team looked narrowly at their police IDs. "I mean, you couldn't do any of the ordinary things, could you? There'd always be the worry you'd be kidnapped, or stalked by someone desperate for money."

Overhearing this, one of the guards, who wore a badge on the pocket of his gray uniform declaring his name to be Ledmark, grinned. "Reckon I could put up with the inconvenience myself," he said. "Like they say, money mightn't buy happiness, but it sure makes misery more bearable."

"You armed?" said the other man, his flat face expressionless. His name tag read Gallagher.

Bourke spread his arms. "Not today, Mr. Gallagher. Going to search me?"

Bourke's tone was bantering, and Carol had to smile at his surprise when the second guard patted him down.

"I'm wearing a sub-compact Glock," she said. Her well-cut jacket hid the outlines of the weapon nestled in its concealed waist holster.

Gallagher seemed about the run his hands over her, too, but Ledmark gave a quick shake of his head. "Inspector Ashton won't be surrendering her gun."

Gallagher accompanied them to the front door of the graceless sandstone house, which had apparently been designed by an architect who valued substance over style. There they were met by yet another guard, this time a woman with a flinty face. "I'll take you through to Mr. Rule's assistant."

In a dourly-furnished drawing room, Thurmond Rule's assistant greeted them with a flicker of a smile. "My name is Hector Paz. I'm delighted to meet you, Inspector Ashton." He shook hands briefly with Carol, then Bourke. "Sergeant Bourke," he said, "I'm afraid you won't be able to accompany the Inspector when she meets Mr. Rule, but I'm sure you'll be comfortable waiting here. I'll arrange for refreshments."

Paz spoke with a slight foreign accent that gave his words an exotic flavor. He was slightly shorter than Carol, and dressed in an undoubtedly expensive beige suit, crisp white shirt and red tie. He had lustrous dark eyes and black hair slicked back over a finely boned skull. Physically he was well-covered, but not fat. Something about him reminded Carol of a cat. Perhaps it was the way he watched them closely with a calm, uninvolved gaze—or maybe it was the impression she had that underneath his cool, unhurried manner lay taut purpose.

A woman in a pale green nurse's uniform entered the room so silently she was almost beside them before Carol was aware of her presence. She quickly looked at each of them, then, hands clasped, said to Paz, "Mr. Rule has had his medication. He will see his visitor now."

"My wife, Juanita," Paz said. "Juanita, meet Inspector Ashton and Sergeant Bourke."

"Welcome," she said with a nervous smile. She spoke with a cadence similar to Paz, and had the same dark hair and deep brown eyes as her husband, but she was slightly built, and his manner of cool watchfulness was absent, being replaced with an anxious attentiveness.

Leaving his wife to attend to Bourke, Hector Paz led Carol down a wide corridor hung with oil paintings in heavy, dark frames. "All originals, of course," he said with pride. "There are galleries that would kill to get a chance to select from this collection." He spoke as if he were the owner of these particular works of art himself.

Paz ushered her through double doors into what appeared to be a library. The walls were lined with enclosed shelves holding countless leather-bound volumes. Heavy furniture sat stolidly on a thick maroon carpet. Sun poured through French windows, heating the room. Even so, a substantial fire crackled in the huge fireplace dominating one wall.

Carol's attention went immediately to the man seated by the fire. The last time she'd seen him was on television six months before. It

11

was a shock to contrast that dynamic figure to the shrunken man before her. She recalled he'd been making appearances in selected programs to refute persistent rumors of serious illness, laughing scornfully at any suggestions that he was losing his grip and his companies' share prices were being affected by any perception that Rule's steady hand on the corporate tiller was failing.

Then it had seemed a ridiculous concept—Rule's ruddy face, thick, iron-gray hair, strong, muscular body, plus the confident tone of his bass voice, had painted a picture of vibrant health.

Now she could see there must have been truth in the rumors. Thurmond Rule had lost considerable weight. His face was haggard, his eyes sunken. His hair seemed thinner, grayer, and his previous vigor entirely dissipated. He was propped up in a black leather armchair, a tartan blanket across his knees, looking more like an invalid than a powerful captain of business.

He waved away Paz's attempts to introduce Carol. "I know who she is. Now leave us."

After Paz had shut the doors behind him, Rule indicated a heavy lounge chair matching the one in which he was slumped. "Sit down over there, opposite me."

It was unpleasantly hot in the room, and Carol would have preferred to be farther from the fire, but courtesy demanded she comply. "I'm so sorry for your loss," she said, seating herself. "Please accept my condolences." He ducked his head in acknowledgment.

Carol couldn't tell if grief or illness had transformed his face into this disconcerting pale, gaunt mask. As though reading her thoughts, Rule said, "I'm much changed, as you can see." His voice had lost its former resonance and was a brittle sound in the quiet room. "This sickness is a temporary thing, Inspector, and I'd request you not mention how I look to anyone."

"I won't, of course."

"I have your word on that, I trust. Although I'm well on the road to recovery, my enemies in the business world would love to spread lies about how old Rule is dying." He coughed, a harsh hacking sound, wiped the back of his hand across his mouth, then continued, "The treatments are worse than the complaint. That's why I look like hell at the moment."

Leaning back, apparently exhausted, Rule closed his eyes. "Tell me about the accident."

"You've seen our reports."

"Yes, yes . . ." He waved a weary hand. "What I want is your account, Inspector." He opened his heavy-lidded eyes. "You're supposed to be among the best the Police Service has to offer." A softly contemptuous laugh followed. "Not that this is necessarily a high recommendation. I'm sure you know Martina had her run-ins with you people. I've always found cops don't hesitate to lie when it suits them."

Disregarding this comment, Carol briefly went through the details of his daughter's death and the steps taken to investigate the incident. She noted both Sid Hawkins, the driver of the truck, and Liam Doherty, the witness, had been closely checked and seemed above-board. Hawkins made a reasonable living running his own business as a handyman doing home repairs. Doherty was a clerk in an electrical wholesalers. There was no indication the two men knew each other, or that either of them had ever met the victim.

To cover every possible angle, Carol had even checked the whereabouts of Henry Courtauld, the man Martina Rule had sent to hospital in the nightclub brawl which had led to her arrest. He'd recovered completely from the concussion and was at present in Britain completing a course at the London School of Economics.

Rule, who'd had his eyes closed during her account, opened them to say, "So you've no doubt the coroner at the inquest will find it was an accident?"

"I believe that's what the ruling will be."

He gave a non-committal grunt, then said, "I've had Fred Verrell look into it. Did you know that?"

Fred Verrell was a high-profile private investigator who special-ized in the problems of the rich and famous. A flamboyant figure who was usually seen with his poodle, Nero, under one arm, Verrell was frequently featured in the media, arguably enjoying more public recognition than some of the celebrities he served.

"Mr. Verrell did contact me about your daughter's death."

Carol didn't add that Verrell's bluster had infuriated her. She had run up against the private detective in other cases, and thoroughly detested his style of operation. Although unfailingly obsequious when dealing with anyone more powerful or famous than himself, Verrell changed to an intimidating bully with those he deemed less significant. In his previous interactions with Carol, Verrell had alternated between sly innuendo—blondes with green eyes turned him on, he'd advised her more than once—and loudmouthed demands for information.

Obviously Rule picked up something in Carol's tone, because he gave a short bark of laughter. "Bit of a bastard, eh? But he's effective. Sure he skates close to illegality at times, but Verrell gets the job done, and that's all that interests me."

"Has he reported to you on this matter?"

Rule nodded. "Verrell agrees with you. Confirms it was a stupid accident. Martina always was careless. Armored by my money, she thought she was immortal."

"Again, Mr. Rule, please accept my condolences." Impatient to end the interview, Carol slid forward in her chair, signaling her intention to stand. "I don't believe there's anything else I can tell you."

He shook his head wearily. "You're right. There's nothing to add to the hard fact my daughter is dead." Pressing a button on an intercom, he said, "Hector? Inspector Ashton is leaving."

As Carol stood, he fixed her with a probing look. "I don't imagine you disappointed your parents, did you?"

"I hope not."

He grunted. "I've no illusions about my daughter, Inspector. My wife died when Martina was ten. I spent as much time with Martina as business would allow, but have to admit I was a neglectful father.

She grew up to be grasping and ungrateful. Money, money, money—that's all she wanted from me. And I gave her whatever she wanted."

As if in his own defense, he added after a moment, "Since my son disappeared all those years ago, Martina was the only family I had left."

Carol vaguely remembered the story: Eric Rule had mysteriously vanished in a remote part of Western Australia. His father had offered a huge reward and financed extensive searches, but no trace of his son had ever been found.

Rule cleared his throat. "It's a hard thing to have your children die before you. A hard thing."

With a pang, Carol thought of her own son, David. He was a teenager now, filled with the typical confidence of his peers that they were immune from harm. "You have my deepest sympathy, Mr. Rule," she said, hoping her sincerity would shine through the commonplace words.

He smiled, and she saw a flash of the former robust Thurmond Rule. "Thank you, Inspector. I appreciate you saying that."

The last sight Carol had of Thurmond Rule was a frail figure, dominated by the sturdy outlines of the chair in which he was slumped. Two weeks later Rule died in his sleep of advanced pancreatic cancer. His obituaries were glowing, his erstwhile enemies having nothing but the most laudatory things to say about the powerful businessman they'd envied and feared.

The media took the opportunity to recycle the mystery of Eric Rule's baffling disappearance. The son had shown very little interest in his father's business empire, instead intending to become a naturalist specializing in conservation. Martina Rule had been three when her half brother, twenty-two, and sole offspring of Thurmond Rule's first marriage, had set off into the wastes of Western Australia's forbidding Gibson Desert as part of a scientific expedition mapping the distribution of a rare reptile, the Great Desert Skink. Eric had been dropped off alone at an isolated point to set up cameras and humane traps, one of many such spots being established by the expedition members. A sudden sandstorm had blown up, delaying his pick-up by several hours. When the desert terrain vehicle returned to the spot, Eric Rule was nowhere to be found. A search was immediately instituted, but the wind had destroyed any tracks made by Eric's boots or any other vehicle that might have been in the area.

Thurmond Rule had spent a not-so-small fortune looking for his son, but to no avail. Twenty years ago, Eric Rule had vanished into the silent wastes of Gibson Desert's undulating sand plains, never, apparently, to be seen again. In the succeeding years, every now and then an article or television program would resurrect the story. Then there'd be a new crop of people claiming to have seen Eric Rule anywhere from Sweden to Chile. Spurious claims would be made for the still-extant reward. Theories would be floated that Eric had been abducted by aliens, or he was married with six children and living under a false name in Blackpool, England, or buried in a lonely desert grave, victim of a remote-area serial killer.

Eric had been declared officially dead more than a decade ago, which left Martina as Thurmond Rule's only close blood relative. Rule's last will and testament was a simple one, naming his daughter as sole heir to his entire estate. As Martina Rule had predeceased her father, and Rule had failed to alter his bequest, at his death no valid will existed.

Rule's only sister had succumbed to leukemia when only twelve. Both his former wives were deceased. With no close relatives available to inherit, the probate court appointed Rule's solicitors to handle the estate's affairs and to seek out more distant kin who might have a claim to the Rule billions. Naturally this generated intense media interest, so the search was widely publicized.

Although Carol didn't follow the story closely, over the next few months she noted with wry amusement the astonishing number of so-called relatives who surfaced in the media, each and every one claiming kinship to the late billionaire. Most were almost immediately discredited by Slessor, Slessor, Dunkling & Gold, Thurmond Rule's solicitors. An old, well-established firm, their probity was beyond reproach. Advertisements seeking possible heirs appeared in all major newspapers throughout Australia, and similar efforts were made in the United States and Britain, as Rule's mother had been Scottish, his father American.

Carol found this far-ranging search for Rule heirs only mildly diverting, and had hardly devoted more than a passing thought to the situation until she received a phone call from the States.

She'd come early to the office, having only made a slight dent in the work she'd taken home to wade through. *I should have accepted Ren's offer,* she thought as she unpacked her bulging briefcase. The chance to become a full partner in a highly successful private investigation firm had been very tempting, but in the end she'd decided to stay with the Police Service. As a police officer she had authority and power an ordinary citizen did not enjoy. When it came down to it, Carol found herself unwilling to relinquish the clout her position gave her. Still, at times like this she wondered if she'd made the right choice.

Carol was counting on at least an hour without interruptions, and was about to start a determined effort to at least temporarily win the paper wars when her phone rang. With a resigned sigh, she picked up the receiver.

Before she could speak, a forceful male voice asked, "Is that Inspector Ashton? Carol Ashton?" The accent had a twang, the tone was impatient.

"This is Carol Ashton."

"Chuck Inman here, calling from Houston, Texas. Australia's to hell and gone, isn't it? What are you—twelve, thirteen hours behind us?"

Carol took a measure of satisfaction in saying, "Actually, Mr. Inman, Australia is ahead of Houston, Texas. It's already the next day, here."

"That so? Whatever, I've got some information you'll want to know."

"And this is in reference to . . . ?"

"Thurmond Rule. The Aussie magnate. You wouldn't want to know how much trouble I had finding out your name. You were in charge of the investigation of his daughter's death, weren't you?"

"I did investigate Martina Rule's fatal accident. Is that what you're calling about?"

"Indirectly. You see, with Martina out of the way, it means I'm one of Thurmond Rule's heirs." Inman gave a short laugh. "Before you say, *Oh, yeah?* let me tell you that unlike most of the would-bes, I'm the genuine article."

Carol looked sourly at the pile of papers in front of her. She had to review several things before a budget meeting that morning. "I believe you should be talking to Mr. Rule's solicitors. They're handling the estate. I'd be pleased to give you contact details."

"Been there, done that," Inman declared brusquely. "This is about something else."

"A police matter?"

"Well, yeah, if you call murder a police matter."

CHAPTER THREE

Later that morning, while waiting for Mark Bourke to get back to her on Chuck Inman and the reliability of his assertions, Carol made another attempt to identify areas where she could shave expenditures. Money was very tight in all government departments, and as law enforcement absorbed a large chunk of the state's resources, urgent instructions to find cost-cutting strategies had filtered down the Police Service chain of command to Carol's level.

She was interrupted several times by phone calls, so when it rang yet again she snatched up the receiver with an impatient sigh. "Carol Ashton."

"I hope you don't use that tone with everyone, Carol."

Carol smiled. "Aunt Sarah. You're back." She visualized her rather chubby aunt, no doubt wearing one of her signature overalls in some blindingly bright color, sitting on Carol's back deck in dappled sunshine. She'd stay with Carol for a few days before returning to her own home in the Blue Mountains.

"Wonderful trip. Most successful in every way."

Carol said, "And you didn't get arrested?"

This got a disdainful snort. "Carol, you worry far too much. The Eco-Crones did have a little adventure in Thailand, I admit, when Lillian was taken away by some officious officer. We got her back pretty soon, not a bit the worse for wear."

Recently recovered from an operation for breast cancer, Aunt Sarah had barely completed her first scheduled check-up—mercifully clear—before embarking on an overseas tour of South-East Asia with members of her Eco-Crones ecology group, who were entertaining thoughts of expanding into an international organization of older women devoted to saving the environment.

Carol had had severe misgivings about the trip, and not because of her aunt's health, which had returned to its usual vigor. The problem was Aunt Sarah's enthusiasm at public demonstrations. Arrested on several occasions, her aunt had gone cheerfully, wearing such detentions as a badge of honor. All Carol's horror stories of hellhole foreign jails had not fazed Aunt Sarah, who had airily waved such concerns away, observing, "In Asia they revere the older woman. Something Western countries could well learn."

They chatted for a few minutes, then Aunt Sarah said, "You're busy, of course, so I won't keep you. See you this evening. We may be eating out, as I've checked your cupboards, Carol, and as usual, healthy foods are conspicuous by their absence."

"I'm shopping on the way home."

"Pick me up, first," said her aunt. "I don't trust you to choose the right things."

As she put down the receiver, Mark Bourke came into her office. "Wonder of wonders, it's still alive, Carol," he said with mock surprise.

They both surveyed the indoor plant sitting on the windowsill. Its abundant green leaves were glossy and it seemed to be flourishing, even though direct light was largely blocked by the building next door.

"Why wouldn't it be?" Carol inquired. "I remember to water it regularly. Besides, as my Aunt Sarah says, you can't kill a philodendron with an ax."

Bourke threw up his hands. "This toxic working environment could shrivel the hardiest plant. The wonder is, *we* survive."

"Much though I'd love to discuss the welfare of indoor plants with you, Mark, I've got a budget meeting coming up, so let's get on with it. What did you find out?"

Bourke took out his ever-present notebook and flipped it open. "Checked with Slessor, Slessor, Dunkling and Gold. Chuck Inman's an American citizen. He's registered as a claimant and he looks to have a good chance of proving a valid relationship, as it appears his great-grandfather on his mother's side was a Rule. Also registered was one Fancee Porter of Austin, Texas. After a bit of a hassle I managed to speak to Ambrose Slessor himself. That's the second Slessor—the first one, his father, is long gone. Anyway, Slessor assured me he had no idea Ms. Porter was reportedly deceased."

"And feedback from the States?"

Bourke grinned. "I got an earful. Both the Houston and the Austin cops are very aware of Charles James Inman. He's been raising merry hell about Fancee Porter and how her death has to be suspicious, but no one's buying it. The Austin police say it was a simple single-vehicle traffic accident. She'd been drinking at a bar, and driving home ran off the road and smacked into a tree."

"Apparently Chuck Inman knows better."

"I'd have kept quiet, if I'd been him," Bourke declared. "Hey, if I were heir to a fortune, and some other claimant got killed, I'd be thinking good-oh, there's one less rival for the cash."

As if on cue the phone rang, and Chuck Inman's strident tones came down the line. "Inspector Ashton? "You've had time to check, so now you know I was telling you God's truth."

Carol put on the speaker phone, so Bourke could listen in. She said, "A woman named Fancee Porter was killed in a car accident in Austin last week, and Thurmond Rule's solicitors have confirmed she was registered as a claimant to the estate. That said, I fail to see why the homicide squad here in Sydney should be involved."

Inman made an exasperated sound. "Weren't you listening when we spoke earlier? Let me put it simply. Someone's planning to remove the competition, one by one. First Martina Rule, then Fancee Porter. The Lord knows who's next." Aggrieved, he added, "It could be *me*."

Carol checked her watch. Her meeting was scheduled in fifteen minutes, and she still hadn't reviewed all the relevant papers. She said in a brisk, let's-get-on-with-it tone, "Mr. Inman, if you have hard evidence you're in danger, you should go straight to the authorities in your own country."

"I've got nothing specific. Yet." His voice growing more belligerent, he went on, "Are you telling me, Inspector, you don't intend to do anything about this? What about Fancee Porter's murder? Isn't it your duty to investigate crime?"

Bourke made a face and rolled his eyes. Carol grinned at his droll expression, but made sure her amusement didn't show in her voice as she replied, "Even if Ms. Porter's death does turn out to be murder, Mr. Inman, not only does the Sydney Police Service have no jurisdiction, we have no reason to be involved. Ms. Porter is an American citizen, not an Australian. It's entirely up to the police in Austin to take any action."

Inman was not impressed. "Just wait til they start dying in Australia," he said. "*Then* you'll be interested!"

● ● ●

Carol returned from the budget meeting full of resigned irritation. Superintendent Edgar had made his usual call for loyalty and sacrifice in these hard times. Each squad was to find ways to economize even further without compromising standards. Overtime and travel expenses were to be strictly limited. All this to operate within what Carol considered a totally inadequate budget, considering the growing burden counter-terrorism measures had imposed. As with all other squads, expenses in homicide were to be tightly monitored. Detailed expenditure reports were to be filled in, and any costs outside the ordinary had to be approved by superiors. Carol was convinced the whole system would be a management nightmare.

She was pleasantly surprised to find special agent Leota Woolfe sitting in her office, her smile very white against her dark skin.

"Leota! How delightful. First Aunt Sarah safely back from travels abroad, and now you."

Leota got up to give her a quick embrace. "I've something important to discuss with you."

"When are you going back to Canberra?"

While taking a course at Quantico, Carol had met Leota, a high-ranking FBI agent. There had been instant attraction between them and subsequently Leota had wrangled a transfer to Australia, where she acted as liaison between the two governments on counter-terrorism. She regularly returned to the States for briefings, and as her base was in Australia's capital, Canberra, her time with Carol was restricted to a few days here or there.

"I've got three days in Sydney. I'm really tired, so I'll crash at the hotel tonight, but how about dinner tomorrow?"

"It's a date. But don't keep me waiting—what do you want to discuss?"

Leota gave her a long, level look. "I've been recalled to the States."

"Recalled?" Seeing Leota's serious expression, she added, "Do you mean permanently?"

"Looks that way."

"When?"

"Soon. I have to show my replacement the ropes, so we're looking at two, maybe three months."

Carol sat down. "That complicates things."

Leota leaned over to kiss her cheek. "We'll talk about it tomorrow."

After she'd gone, Carol sat pensively staring at nothing. It wasn't that Leota hadn't floated the idea of returning to America before, but the issue had been something Carol was content to push aside until it came to the crunch.

The crunch, it seemed, had arrived. And decisions were being forced upon her—decisions she was reluctant to make.

● ● ●

Although Carol didn't subscribe to Chuck Inman's theory someone had embarked on a scheme to bump off would-be heirs, the issue nagged at her. She pictured Thurmond Rule as she had last seen him, with cancer eating away his desiccated body. There had been no family members to mitigate the loneliness of Rule's last days. He had died surrounded by people paid to be with him. In some odd way, Carol felt a responsibility toward the dead man. She checked a number, hesitated, then called.

She was efficiently and politely grilled by a personal assistant before being given an appointment with Mr. Slessor later that day. She worked through her lunchtime to assuage the tinge of guilt that she was wasting valuable time by following up on something so tenuous.

Slessor, Slessor, Dunkling & Gold were situated in an historic sandstone building in Philip Street. The building's elegant façade was echoed in the solicitors' rooms, which were tastefully understated. There was an atmosphere of hushed accomplishment, as though the unassuming, yet clearly expensive furnishings reflected the assured successes of the firm.

Carol was ushered into Ambrose Slessor's office by a middle-aged woman with impeccable grooming who moved so smoothly she seemed to glide over the thick carpet. The solicitor rose to greet her in a resonant bass voice too large for his slight frame. Slessor's subtly pin-striped suit and his tie of an exclusive private school were the expected uniform for a man in his position. He was a small, delicately-boned man with a slender neck, an overlarge head, and a mustache so thin it might as well have been drawn on with an eyebrow pencil.

"How may I help you, Inspector Ashton?" he asked as they settled down in his traditional lawyer's office with dark legal tomes lining the shelves and tasteful etchings of indeterminate subjects on the walls.

"To be truthful, Mr. Slessor, I'm not altogether sure. Perhaps you're aware I was in charge of the investigation of Martina Rule's death."

Slessor's head bobbed on the thin stalk of his neck. "Indeed. Mr. Rule did have occasion to mention to me he was satisfied you had carried out an exemplary investigation."

"This morning I had a call from a Mr. Chuck Inman of Houston, Texas."

"Ah, yes. Mr. Inman."

Carol's lips quirked at the wary note in Slessor's voice. She said, "I suspect you've been exposed to Mr. Inman's conspiracy theory?"

"He did mention it. Frankly, I paid very little heed to his conjectures. The whole thing seemed entirely too paranoid."

"I'm inclined to agree," said Carol. "Even so, although the inquest determined that Martina Rule's death was an accident, I feel I should make sure there are no loose ends."

"Excellent!" Loose ends clearly were not something of which Slessor approved. "One cannot, I've found, be too careful."

"I believe your firm is the clearing house, as it were, for all the claims on Thurmond Rule's estate."

"You are correct. The court has set as our task the winnowing of the chaff from the grain." He made a moderate snorting sound Carol decided was his version of a laugh, then remarked, "If I might make an observation, Inspector, there is much chaff, and very little grain."

"Mr. Inman is grain?"

He folded his short-fingered hands on the blotter in front of him. "It's conceivable," he said with lawyerly caution.

"And Fancee Porter?"

"She did appear to be a legitimate relative."

"And apart from these two, there are others who seem to have genuine claims on the estate?"

"There are," he conceded.

"May I ask how many?"

Slessor pursed his lips, apparently considering the ramifications of answering her question. "Of course I can't reveal names . . ."

"Would there be two? Three? I'm just looking for an indication."

"At this point, six, apart from Mr. Inman and Miss Porter." He leaned forward with an expression of gravity. "Needless to say, I would ask that you keep this entirely confidential."

"How do you ascertain if an individual is genuinely related to Thurmond Rule?"

He looked faintly offended, as though Carol might be criticizing the firm's procedures. "Each claim is vetted stringently. Apart from inquiries we make ourselves, we use the services of an eminent genealogist. We also employ a very reputable firm to investigate each person asserting kinship."

"The name of the firm?" When he hesitated, Carol smiled at him. "Surely, Mr. Slessor, that cannot be something you'd withhold from the police."

"Downing and Pate," he said. "No doubt you've heard of the company."

She had indeed. Ren Downing of Downing & Pate was the person who had previously offered her the partnership she'd turned down. "I know Ren Downing personally," she said. "I agree his investigative firm has the highest reputation."

Obviously pleased with this validation, Slessor sat back in his chair. Carol said, "It's highly unlikely, but I'm wondering if there's any pattern of unusual deaths in the claimants."

Slessor's meager mustache twitched. "Really, Inspector, I'm very surprised that you give credence to Mr. Inman's imaginative ideas."

"A loose end that may need tying, Mr. Slessor."

Somewhat mollified by Carol's analogy, the solicitor said, "Under the circumstances, I can see no harm in making a general comment. In the course of ordinary existence, people die. We hadn't been officially advised of Miss Porter's death in Austin, but no doubt this information would have been forthcoming. As far as other claimants are concerned, yes, there has been one death in the last few weeks." He shook his over-large head. "Regrettably, the person took his own life."

"This possible heir, was he Australian?"

"Oh, yes. He lived in Sydney."

"His name?" She put up her hand before the solicitor could make the objection she saw coming. "Mr. Slessor, I should be able to put this whole matter to rest before Chuck Inman has a chance to go public."

She was amused to see she'd played this card well. "Go public?" he repeated in tones of abhorrence. Without further protest, he gave her the name.

Before she left, she asked a question that had been puzzling her. "Why didn't Mr. Rule make a new will after his daughter died?"

"Oh, believe me, Inspector, I tried to persuade him to do just that." He gave a rueful smile. "I did my best, but failed. Had I succeeded, we wouldn't now be in the unfortunate position of relying on the probate court to distribute his considerable assets to whichever claimants are deemed apposite. Sadly, Mr. Rule was not only prostrated by grief over the loss of his daughter, he was also heavily sedated most of the time. And add to that the fact he refused to admit he was dying . . ."

Slessor's expression reflected his lawyerly frustration at his intransigent client.

"What happens if heirs to his fortune die before the matter comes before the court?"

"Strictly speaking, Inspector, in difficult situations like this, no one *is* an heir until the court determines that particular individual has a valid claim on the estate. Should such a person predecease the court's ruling, his or her relatives might consider legal action, but the cost of so doing is not inconsiderable, and the outcome by no means certain."

Slessor ostentatiously consulted his gold wristwatch. Carol obediently rose to her feet. "Thank you, Mr. Slessor, for your time and your help."

"Please don't hesitate to contact me if I can be of further assistance."

"Thank you," said Carol, amused by the contradictory message he conveyed with a slight lift of an eyebrow and a twitch of his slender mustache. It was clear Slessor hoped this would be their first, and only meeting.

● ● ●

"Anne?"

Anne Newsome looked up from her desk with a grin. "Boss?"

The young constable was one of the most promising officers Carol had ever had under her command. With clear olive skin and curly brown hair, she projected an aura of wholesome competence. Carol had never heard her swear, but Anne had had no trouble fitting in with her often foul-mouthed colleagues. Moreover, she kept herself extremely fit, was not daunted by a constantly heavy workload, and exhibited a keen analytical mind. Carol was particularly pleased with the way Anne had continued to develop her interviewing skills, particularly with difficult witnesses.

Carol said, "Where are you with the Holland case?"

"I've just completed the report. Having a full confession makes it pretty simple, really."

In this homicide the victim and his murderer were close friends who'd been drinking together. Something had sparked a fight, they'd got into a physical confrontation, and a sharp kitchen knife had been there for the grabbing. It was typical of many homicides Carol had investigated—in one hotheaded moment, two lives had been destroyed, two families devastated.

Carol handed Anne a thin file. "There hasn't been an inquest yet, but a guy called Ian Stewart apparently killed himself. It's Wally Ford's case, but I've taken it out of his hands for the moment. I want you to look through the file, make a few phone calls, then give me your assessment."

"You don't think it's suicide?"

"It's probably what it appears to be, but there may be a connection to another death. I'm not saying any more, Anne. I want your unbiased opinion."

"And what if there is something suspicious?"

Carol grinned. "Then things will get interesting, fast."

● ● ●

Aunt Sarah, an energetic figure with a corona of white hair, zipped along the aisles of fresh produce. Carol followed on behind, watching her loading the shopping trolley with more food than Carol could consume in a month. "It's no use getting all those fresh vegetables, aunt," she protested. "I'll never get to eat them."

"You eat vegetables and fruit when I'm around."

"That's because I haven't got a choice."

"Spinach," said Aunt Sarah, grabbing a bunch and inspecting it closely. "Excellent stuff." She looked narrowly at Carol. "When was the last time you ate spinach?"

"I can't quite remember."

"I'd venture to say, Carol, it was the last time I stayed with you."

Aware a passing shopper was grinning, having obviously overheard, Carol tried to end the subject. "I'd venture to say you're right."

They moved on to the fruit section. Her aunt examined a pineapple meticulously, replaced it and selected another. "Steamed vegetables," she said, "followed by a fresh fruit salad. How does that sound for dinner?"

Sending a critical glance at Aunt Sarah's plump form, Carol asked, "Is that what you'd be eating if you were at home?"

"Heavens no, dear. I'd be more likely to have pasta with a delicious meat sauce. But then, I have a balanced diet. *You* do not." A sudden smile lit her face. "Oh, all right. I'll cook something sinful for you tonight, but tomorrow is another story."

"I'll be out for dinner tomorrow, and probably won't be home at all, if that's okay. Leota's in town for a couple of days." Carol hesitated, then said, "She's been recalled to the States."

Aunt Sarah put down a mango. "You mean she's going back to America for good?"

"Yes."

After a pause, her aunt said, "Has Leota asked you to go with her?"

"We haven't discussed it."

Aunt Sarah seemed to have lost her zest for shopping. "Let's go," she said.

All the way home she avoided the subject of Leota, prattling cheerfully about her portrait by Yancey Blake, which was to be entered for the prestigious Archibald Prize. Carol had seen the just-completed painting, and wasn't quite sure whether she liked it, although it was certainly striking. The artist had captured Aunt Sarah as ardent Eco-Crone, radiating energy and commitment. Behind her a vivid assemblage of diverse flora and fauna crowded the canvas.

Carol was only half-paying attention to her aunt's chatter when a name caught her attention. "What did you say?"

"Rude of you not to listen closely, darling. I was saying I've suggested to Sybil that she and Yancey hold a cocktail party for a private viewing of my portrait. I know the Eco-Crones would come down to Sydney like a shot." With rising enthusiasm she added, "We could make the viewing an environmental fund-raiser."

"We? You're not including me in this, are you? I'm snowed under at work."

"It wouldn't take much to organize, Carol. Just a few plates of savories and lots of red and white wine." Aunt Sarah shot Carol a guileless smile. "Perhaps you and Sybil could work on the function together, dear."

"Not a chance."

"Tsk," said her aunt, "I thought you and Sybil were well on the way to becoming friends again."

"Of course we're friends. It's just I don't have time to spare for organizing a cocktail party," said Carol, knowing her first statement was close to a lie, the second the unvarnished truth.

Sybil had once meant so much to her. And time hadn't entirely healed the emotional wounds on Carol's side the way conventional wisdom said it would. It was nothing to do with the fact Sybil and Yancey were together. It was simply that friendship between Carol and Sybil had proved impossible to establish. Carol assured herself she'd tried several times. It had never worked. And it never would work. No matter what Aunt Sarah ardently wished, friendship was not now, and never could be an option. Distant caring was as close as Carol expected to get.

CHAPTER FOUR

The next morning Carol was in a little later than usual, having made a stop on the way to see Terry Roham in hospital. It was a duty visit, as she was his superior officer, but she also found to her surprise she was developing kinder feelings toward a young constable who'd previously tried her patience to the limit.

Terry had been critically injured when deliberately run down by a vehicle. His full recovery had been delayed by a persistent infection in his shattered leg. For a while it seemed this had been overcome, but now he was back in hospital because the infection had flared up again.

Terry's brash, super-confident nature had been softened by the ordeal he'd gone through, so he didn't entirely hide from Carol his fears he might not recover sufficiently to return to active duty. Carol had been reassuring, and left him more cheerful than she had found him.

She was thinking of Terry when she called Anne Newsome into her office. It had been rivalry with Anne, plus a desire to impress Carol with his abilities, that had led Terry into the confrontation that nearly cost him his life.

"I saw Terry this morning," she said when Anne appeared.

"A crowd of us are going tonight. How is he?"

"Terry's hiding it, but he's worried his career's over. Be suitably bracing, Anne. Terry's young and strong, and there's no reason he won't make a full recovery."

Anne shook her head. "I just can't imagine what it must feel like to be that close to dying."

Carol knew. It was an experience that could not be shared, so there was no point in discussing it. Switching to business, she said, "You've looked at the Stewart file. What do you think? An adequate investigation?"

When Anne looked uncomfortable, Carol added, "I want you to be frank. If the investigating officer has screwed up, I need to know."

Carol's opinion of Sergeant Wally Ford was not high. She judged him as a barely adequate homicide officer. He was pleasant enough, but was also lazy, so he needed close supervision.

Anne hesitated, then said, "I suppose I'd say it was a fairly perfunctory investigation, but that's probably all it needed to be. A simple suicide, the sort that happens every day. Don't think there's any doubt the coroner will find Ian Stewart took his own life."

Carol had glanced at the file before giving it to Anne. The report detailed the method Stewart had used to kill himself. He had taken a quantity of Valium tablets with alcohol, and when the tranquilizers took effect and he became drowsy, had fastened a plastic bag over his head, securing it around his neck with two thick rubber bands to prevent air entering. Then, either unconscious or perhaps

33

still semi-aware of his surroundings, he'd breathed the last of the oxygen in the bag. Within a few short minutes he was dead. It was a method, Carol recalled, advocated by a British writer and proponent of "rational suicide."

His body had been discovered by a friend, John Hansen, who'd become concerned when Stewart failed to meet him on schedule. Stewart had been lying peacefully on his bed. A short note on the side table was his last communication with the world.

"What do your instincts tell you, Anne?"

Anne made a face. "It's probably what it seems—a suicide. Stewart was a bit of a loner. He was a long-time widower, no kids. Didn't have a lot of friends, lived with his sister-in-law, Gaye Mason. But also, he'd never shown any signs of deep depression, and the friend who found him says in his statement he was astonished to find Stewart had killed himself. I called Ms. Mason this afternoon, and she too, said the same—she couldn't believe it."

"The nearest and dearest are often astonished," Carol observed. "Not knowing the real thoughts and feelings of someone close to them, they're dumbfounded when the person commits suicide."

"Take a look at the note," said Anne. "Nothing original there—it's generic as you can get."

Carol flipped pages until she found the photocopy of the suicide note Stewart had left. Only the scrawled signature was by hand—the main part, a scant two sentences, had been printed out.

I'm very sorry but I can't take it any more. Please forgive me.

The signature was just his first name, Ian.

"He typed it on his computer then printed it on a laser printer," said Anne. I'm wondering why didn't he write the whole thing by hand. Why go to all that trouble for thirteen words?"

"You've counted them?"

Anne grinned. "Not a lucky number, thirteen."

"In this case apparently not," said Carol dryly. "What about the signature?"

"Gaye Mason says it's her brother-in-law's writing, but a short word like *Ian* can't be hard to forge."

"So your theory is . . . ?"

"I don't actually have a theory, just a feeling that maybe there's a few more questions could have been asked. For instance, where did Stewart get the Valium from?"

Carol flicked through more pages, frowning at Wally Ford's sparse documentation. "He didn't have a doctor's prescription?"

"Seems not. There were a few Valium tablets left in an unmarked bottle on the bedside, but no indication of where they came from."

"Perhaps his sister-in-law was the source?"

Anne shook her head. "No way. I asked her when I called. She's heavily into alternative medicine. Won't have prescription drugs in the house."

"I'll talk to Wally," said Carol. "He may have information in his notes he didn't bother to put in his report."

• • •

"No doubt about it, Stewart offed himself," said Wally Ford. "It's all in my report." He yawned mightily, stretched. He was muscular, but getting soft around the middle. "Got to stop burning the candle at both ends." This with a complacent smile.

Carol had had to wait until late in the morning to catch up with Ford, who apparently saw no need for punctuality when his team leader was off on compassionate leave.

"There's very little in your report," said Carol, her acerbic tone making him blink. She flicked over a page or two. "The bare minimum."

"What more was there to say?" Ford's tone was injured. "The guy killed himself. It's a tragedy, and all that, but no use knocking yourself out over it."

"Your notes," said Carol. "I'd like to see them."

"There's nothing in my notes that isn't in there," he said, indicating the slim folder Carol held. "What's all the fuss about?"

"The man killed himself with Scotch, the prescription drug Valium and a plastic bag," said Carol. "The alcohol and plastic bag are easily obtained, but where did Stewart get the Valium? He had no doctor's prescription for it."

"I dunno. Stole it, borrowed it, bought it on the street . . ."

His attitude was as slapdash as his detective work. Carol looked at him with disgust. "And the note Stewart left?" she said. "Generic clichés, saying nothing."

"Hey," said Wally Ford, "we can't all be Shakespeare, you know."

• • •

It was getting late. Carol wanted to go home to shower and change before meeting Leota. What she might or might not say had bounced around in her head all afternoon. On one hand she couldn't imagine leaving Australia, or the career she had in law enforcement—on the other she felt a tingle of excitement at the thought of another country, familiar yet foreign, and perhaps a new career.

She glared at the files in her in-tray. It seemed she was forever lugging the same ones home, then bringing them back the next day. In a short absence from the room she saw a new file had been added with a note attached: *Urgent. Budget Projections.*

She swore, inadvertently timing this to coincide with the entry of the Commissioner.

"Inspector Ashton . . . Carol. This is a bad time?"

"Not at all, Commissioner."

Carol had had an excellent relationship with the former head of the Police Service, who had been in many respects her mentor. She was still feeling her way with this new man, less than a year in the position, who combined a handsome face with political savvy and a hardnosed reputation. These were helpful attributes for the top job, but she had yet to be convinced he would provide the leadership so urgently required.

The Commissioner didn't waste time with pleasantries. He sat down, waited until she had taken her chair behind her desk, then said, "I had a call from an old friend of mine, Ambrose Slessor. I believe you saw him this afternoon. Something about the Rule estate."

Carol grimaced mentally. She might have known the Commissioner would be mates with the principal partner of one of the best-known legal firms in Sydney.

She said, "I went to see Mr. Slessor because Charles Inman, an American who claims to be a Rule heir, called me early this morning from Houston with information about another claimant who'd died last week in a car accident in Texas. Despite the fact the police found it was a single-vehicle fatal accident, Inman is insisting it's murder. He has the unlikely theory that some unknown person is getting rid of the Rule heirs, one by one."

He nodded, his face impassive. She went on, "Mr. Slessor mentioned someone else on the short list had committed suicide here in Sydney. The death of a second person is probably a coincidence, however I'm looking into it."

"That investigation will be part of a wider inquiry."

Surprised, Carol repeated, "A wider inquiry?"

"I'm setting it in motion today. This is going to be a free-for-all as far as the media's concerned, so I need someone with your fine touch to put out the fires. To start, we have a problem with Inman. He called Ambrose Slessor a short time ago and accused him of mishandling the whole matter of the inheritance. After making some very rash comments about the integrity of the firm, including the allegation Slessor knew more about Martina Rule's death than he was letting on, Inman announced he was flying to Sydney to arrange his own legal representation to protect his interests."

Carol said mildly, "Perhaps that's wise, when there's billions at stake."

He grunted. "I don't see this Yank being the shy, retiring type. He'll get as much publicity as he can. I'm relying on you to handle the situation."

With her workload this was impossible. "Commissioner, I—"

"Hear me out. Thurmond Rule was a close personal friend. My daughter and his went to the same schools. If there's any possibility crimes have been committed, I want to know. I'm taking you off your other cases and giving you any resources you need to mount a full investigation. That includes reviewing Thurmond's death too, although I have no doubt it was a natural one. Take a second look at Martina's accident. Check out the suicide. Do anything else necessary. If there's any substance to this Yank's theory, I'm relying on you to find it."

The Commissioner stood. "Report directly to me." At the door he turned to give her a frosty smile. "I imagine there'll be bitter complaints about the impact this investigation will have on the budget allocation for your department. Anyone with a grievance can see me."

Bemused, Carol sat back in her chair. A few moments ago she'd been grousing to herself about a few files—now she'd been handed a major investigation with the potential to make or break her. Even this early in his term, the Commissioner had not hesitated to deal out severe reprimands to officers who'd embarrassed the Service with public failures. Carol could expect the same career-derailing consequences should she fall short of his expectations.

• • •

Carol had intended to delay discussion of Leota's bombshell news until after dinner, and when the subject came up, to be rational and calm about it, but as soon as she was inside the door of Leota's hotel room and had given her a perfunctory kiss, she heard herself saying, "Tell me what's happening."

"It's quite simple. I'm being recalled to the States." Leota eyed her warily, as though expecting an outburst of protest, or even anger. "You knew it was always a possibility. There was no way I was here permanently."

"Is it a promotion for you?"

"Yes, it is, but that's not relevant."

Carol said, with a grim smile, "Personally, I'd find a promotion very relevant." It was a sore point with her. She could have expected to be Chief Inspector Ashton by now, given her successes. But one catastrophic failure, plus covert opposition from at least one of her superiors, had stalled her at the rank of inspector.

Leota put out her hands in entreaty. "Please believe me, honey, I didn't ask for this to happen. I'm being recalled, promotion or not. I don't have an option."

Carol felt a spurt of anger. "Of course you have an option. You could resign, if needs be."

Leota shook her head slowly. "You know I won't do that. It might sound sappy, but it's patriotism. I'm involved in the security of my country. That means everything to me."

Carol stalked over to the window, and stood looking unseeingly out at the city. After a long pause, she turned to face Leota. "And what are you asking me to do?"

"Carol, I don't want to be without you. I hope you feel the same way. Would you consider coming with me?"

"To the States? To do what? I don't have a green card, so I can't work."

"Something can be arranged."

"Like what?" Carol snapped, feeling resentment corroding her desire to remain cool, composed.

"Whatever you like. I can pull strings. Carol, I don't want to lose you." She gave a rueful laugh. "Bad phrasing. I don't want to lose what we have together."

When Carol didn't respond, Leota continued, "It's a big decision. Hell, it's gigantic, huge, overwhelming. All of the above. Believe me, I know."

"You're saying that because you came to Australia for me. But Leota, it was always temporary, never permanent. Admit it. You always knew you'd be going home. You kept your job, you kept your apartment in Washington."

After another long silence, Leota said, "I know what I'm asking you to give up—your career, your house . . ."

"Sinker."

This brought a reluctant smile to Leota's lips. "You don't have to give up your cat. There's no quarantine for pets entering the States, so you can bring Sinker into the country without a problem."

"And even if I got to the point of agreeing to go, where do you see us living? In your apartment?" Carol visualized the cramped, dark rooms, compared to the sunlit luxury of her own house. "It would be too small."

"Carol, we've both got a lot of thinking to do. We can worry about the details like where we'd live much later. Let's talk more tomorrow."

Carol suddenly felt unutterably tired. "Can we make the whole subject off limits for the rest of the evening?"

"Agreed." Leota smiled, held out her arms. "Let's start again, from the time I opened the door to you."

Carol went willingly to her embrace, wanting the rush of raw desire to wash away the thoughts and feelings that roiled her mind. Tomorrow would be soon enough for hard decisions.

CHAPTER FIVE

Carol played with her gold pen, frowning at the points she'd jotted down. Leaving Leota still sleeping, she'd snatched a cup of coffee at the hotel coffee shop, then come straight to work. It was very early, and pleasingly, the phone hadn't interrupted her once.

She'd headed the page with a large question mark, which, she thought, pretty well summed up how she felt. The first column was *Fors*, the second *Againsts*. So far she had five points in favor of the move: being with Leota; a new, exciting country; new opportunities; new challenges; Sinker can come.

The points against her moving to the States were all to do with what she'd lose—her career, her house, seeing her son grow up, Aunt Sarah's company.

She threw down the pen. It was an impossible situation. She couldn't imagine not having Leota in her life. She couldn't imagine leaving her son, her beloved aunt, her home. Which pain would be the greater? Could there conceivably be any way to determine this before the experience itself?

"You're here bright and early," said Bourke, sticking his head through the door.

"Come in and sit down, Mark. The Commissioner's initiated a major investigation. I'm not altogether sure it's good news, but it's our baby. We're to drop everything and concentrate on any deaths associated with the Rule inheritance."

They spent an hour discussing the logistics. In order for Bourke to be free to collect information about the short list of individuals with legitimate claims to the Rule fortune, much of his current workload would have to be shared amongst the other members of Carol's team, and they were already working close to capacity.

It was all very well, she thought, for the Commissioner to make a grand statement Carol would be relieved of her present cases and given all the resources she needed for the Rule investigation. Although her direct superiors would rubber-stamp the Commissioner's edicts, she fully expected the implementation would be left to her. And Carol no illusions that any of the six other teams in homicide would volunteer to take on more work. It was going to be a matter of trade-offs, promises, and calling in favors owed.

It was therefore a pleasant surprise later that morning to find Superintendent Edgar—a master at squeezing every advantage out of the system—was gung-ho about this new investigation.

Calling her into his office with a deceptively avuncular smile, Edgar said, "Leave the reallocation of your work entirely to me, Carol. I want you free to concentrate fully on the matter at hand."

She was aware this enthusiasm to relieve her of this particular burden was not a demonstration of whole-hearted support from her superior officer. It was dictated by the fact Superintendent Edgar scented yet another opportunity to enhance his career by close association with a high-profile case.

"I want you to report directly to me," he said, smoothing his thick silver-white hair with his habitual grooming gesture. "I'll see to it personally the Commissioner is kept apprised of developments."

"The Commissioner did ask me to report directly to him."

Edgar's bonhomie was replaced with a frown. "I see." He drummed his fingers on his desk. "Of course you must follow the Commissioner's instructions. However, I will require full report on your progress as well."

Carol hid a wry smile. One way or the other, Superintendent Edgar would make this case his own—in name, if not in practice. As always, he would lay claim to successes, and avoid like the plague association with any failures.

● ● ●

While waiting for Bourke's report, Carol decided to tackle the matter of Thurmond Rule, as she agreed with the Commissioner's assertion the billionaire's death was almost certainly a natural one. This should make it a simple matter to check out. She called Ambrose Slessor to ask for the head of Rule's medical team, having no doubt there had been a number of eminent specialists associated with his treatment.

After some delay, Slessor came on the line. He sounded alarmed at her request, and was not appeased by Carol's soothing, "It's merely a routine matter."

"Surely you're not thinking his death was murder!" he exclaimed. "It's preposterous! Mr. Rule died from the ravages of pancreatic cancer."

"Murder?" said Carol, intrigued by Slessor's heated response. "Why would you leap to that conclusion?"

There was a pause. Carol imagined Slessor's large head bobbing on his thin neck as he scrambled to select an appropriate answer.

He said in a much more moderate tone, "Taking into account

what Inman's been saying about Ms. Porter's death, it's not much of a leap to imagine he's making further wild allegations."

"To my knowledge, Mr. Inman has said nothing on the subject."

Placated by Carol's calm statement, Slessor gave her the name and number of Rule's principal physician, Dr. George McMinn.

"Now, if there's nothing else . . ." Plainly he was keen to end the conversation.

"There is one other thing."

"Yes?" Slessor's tone was wary.

"I presume Mr. Rule's nurse dispensed all his medication."

"Indeed. Mrs. Paz was indefatigable." He spoke with more warmth than Carol had yet heard in his voice. "Near the end she was by Mr. Rule's side night and day. She slept in a chair in his room. I could not speak too highly of her professionalism."

"Juanita Paz is originally from another country, isn't she?"

"That's correct. Mrs. Paz and her husband are from Colombia, South America. I believe they emigrated to Australia about thirteen years ago."

"And how did they come to work for Mr. Rule?"

Slessor made an impatient sound, evidently trying to convey to Carol his need to end the call. When she remained silent, he sighed. In a brisk, let's-get-it-over tone, he said, "Some time after arriving here, Hector Paz went to work for Mr. Rule as his personal assistant. Having worked to gain all the required nursing accreditations for this country, Mrs. Paz was employed by one of the major hospitals, and soon attained a senior position. When Mr. Rule was diagnosed with a serious illness requiring constant medical care, it was the obvious move to appoint Juanita Paz as his personal nurse."

"Do you know how I can contact her?"

"Why, she's still at the house. In my role as trustee, I've appointed both Juanita Paz and her husband to act as caretakers, until such time as the courts rule on the distribution of the estate. As you might imagine, there are some extremely valuable artworks, furniture, antiques and the like in the residence. For this reason I've

44

also retained several of the security staff under the direction of David Ledmark, who was Mr. Rule's personal bodyguard before his illness."

Slessor gave her the telephone number of Rule's mansion, and volunteered to advise the staff to cooperate fully with the police. Carol finished the call with the cynical thought the solicitor had made this gesture not out of goodwill, but because he wanted to make sure everyone was circumspect in their responses.

She played telephone tag with Dr. McMinn for several hours, finally getting hold of him in mid-afternoon. The physician confirmed he'd signed the death certificate without hesitation, as Rule had been his patient since the diagnosis of cancer eighteen months before he died. There was not the slightest doubt cancer had brought about his demise. As there was no question about the cause of death, and he'd been under Dr. McMinn's direct care, there had been no suggestion of a post mortem. Following Rule's instructions, his body had been cremated.

"He was a brave man, Inspector. Refused to admit he was dying. Fought to the very last. In some respects that's admirable, but it can lead to much suffering, too."

Carol asked if Rule had been on morphine, and McMinn confirmed he had been. Near the end of Rule's life Juanita Paz had been administering the painkiller every few hours.

After jotting down relevant details, Carol thanked the doctor for his time and rang off. Large doses of morphine administered to a weakening body might well hasten death by a few hours or days. This fact was not generally discussed, but it was an open secret some doctors were complicit in what Carol had heard described as "merciful death."

As she was musing over the issue of compassionate euthanasia, Bourke appeared with his preliminary report. "Slessor, Slessor, Dunkling and Gold were besieged by literally hundreds of people vehemently claiming a blood relationship to Thurmond Rule," he said. "Fortunately for the solicitors, Rule's kin have never been particularly fruitful, so even though the family tree looks like a tangled forest to an amateur like me, apparently it hasn't been all that hard to decide who was a genuine relative. Of course the court will have the final say as to which applicants inherit and how the estate will be divided up."

He handed Carol a blue plastic folder. "The eight distant relatives who made the final list," he said, folding himself neatly into a chair. "Overwhelmingly male—only a couple of women. As of today, there've been two deaths, Fancee Porter in Texas and Ian Stewart here in Sydney. That leaves six to fight over the inheritance."

"You have them in strict alphabetical order, I hope," said Carol, opening the folder.

"Could you doubt it?"

Bourke's zeal for orderliness was a long-standing joke between them. As always, he'd provided a well-organized report in very little time. Biographical details included a photograph of each person, some from passport or driving license records, others from news items.

"This is great, Mark."

"I had a lot of help from Dowling and Pate, specifically Ren Dowling, as he was involved in checking people the solicitors' genealogist believed might genuinely be related to Thurmond Rule. Ren wouldn't let me look at his files, but he was quite okay about answering general questions."

"Did you meet the genealogist?"

"Sure did. Pam Kaye. She's a chirpy little woman with her own thriving business. Who would have thought so many people would be interested in tracing family trees? Pam made a valiant effort to explain the blood links between Rule and each claimant, but lost me once she started in on cousins removed so many times, great-grand-aunts and all that stuff. I'm taking her word for it when she says everyone on the list appears to be a valid heir."

The first in the folder was Jim Flint, twenty. A native of Perth, Western Australia, he had apparently never left the state of his birth until recently, when he moved across country to Sydney in order to pursue his claim. He'd been adopted when a baby, but when eighteen had reunited with his biological mother shortly before she drank herself to death. It was through her he discovered that Rule was a distant relative.

Flint's photograph showed a truculent young man with a heavy jaw and stocky build. "Flint and his girlfriend Kirra are living with his married stepsister and her family, and he's working part-time as a delivery driver," said Bourke. "Nasty piece of work. Drinks too much, then bashes the nearest likely target, often some unfortunate female. Likes roaring around in his souped-up truck. Flint's been arrested several times for assault, drunk driving, and resisting arrest. Completed community service and alcohol counseling in lieu of jail time."

The next would-be heir was Kent Humphries, a flight attendant with Qantas Airways. He'd been born in Britain, but was now a naturalized Australian. He was thirty-eight, unmarried, and when not flying lived in a small apartment block he owned in the Sydney beach suburb of Bondi.

A subtly asymmetrical face stared from his photograph. His mouth was a little crooked, his nose veered off center just slightly, one eyebrow was higher than the other. Carol found the overall effect beguiling. This was the face of a man who seemed to be nursing some humorous, private thought that he might share, if asked by the right person.

"Does Humphries fly the American route?" she asked.

"Bingo, Carol. If there's anything to Inman's story, Kent Humphries might be one who could conceivably be in the vicinity when Fancee Porter died. I haven't been able to check his schedule yet, but I will at the first op."

Third on the list was the man who'd phoned Carol from Houston, Chuck Inman. The information Bourke had was scant and the only photo he'd been able to lift off the Internet was so blurred all Carol could ascertain was that Chuck Inman appeared to be a large man.

"Inman calls himself a businessman," said Bourke. "I get the impression he's been involved in quite a few questionable deals, but I'm still waiting on information from the States."

"What did Ren say about him?"

"Not much. Just that Inman had a clearly valid claim, and that he was quite a character."

"Meaning?"

"A loud Texan, I suppose. You know, the stereotype you see in movies." Bourke leapt up, tugged at the brim of an imaginary cowboy hat, hooked his fingers in his belt, and drawled, "Howdy, ma'am. You're a mighty purty little thang."

"Oh, please!" said Carol, laughing. "Like they say, stick to your day job, fella."

She turned to the next page. "There are two Jordans?"

"Ah," said Bourke. "This is interesting." He pointed to a photograph of a middle-aged man with a doughy face and bleak expression. "That's Nicholas Jordan before his accident. He fell about twenty meters on a construction site a year ago. Now he's comatose and permanently hooked to machines to keep him alive. His long-term prognosis is grim."

Bourke indicated a second photograph, which was of a woman of similar age. She had the same doughy face, but her expression was one of such intense animosity that Carol had the fanciful thought the woman might lean out of the photo and bite Carol's nose.

"She's a beauty," she remarked.

"That's his sister, Sue Jordan. You'll love this, Carol. Last year she legally changed her name by deed poll to Ophelia Rule."

Carol looked up with a grin. "Oh, come on. You're kidding me, Mark. Ophelia Rule?"

"It's not that our Sue's a great fan of Shakespeare's *Hamlet*. It's because she researched the Rules and found Ophelia used to be a common name in the family."

"And that would help her—how?"

"About two years ago, when Sue Jordan discovered she and her

48

brother were related to Thurmond Rule, she started a campaign to be accepted into the bosom of the family."

"How did she find out?" Carol asked.

"About her Rule blood? No idea. I'll follow it up." Characteristically, he stopped to jot down a reminder to himself, then went on, "It'd be nice to think Sue Jordan heard kinship calling, but I suspect the scent of money was the real reason. When Rule didn't deign to reply to her letters or calls, she tried to get to him in person. She was turned away at the gates to his mansion several times, and when she tried accosting him when he made public appearances, his bodyguards made sure she never got close."

"Was she harassing Martina Rule too?"

"It seems she was only interested in the father." Bourke added mockingly, "And very understandable, too, since he was the only billionaire in the family."

"So did Rule and this woman ever meet?"

"Apparently not, in spite of all her efforts. You got to admire the woman—she wasn't easily discouraged. Eventually Rule took out a restraining order against her. She wasn't a bit happy to learn this, and her next move was to instruct a lawyer to take steps to legally change her name to Ophelia Rule, apparently to bolster her claim of being a member of the family. Once she was a Rule in name, she made a concentrated effort to get the media interested in her story of a spurned relative of the famous Thurmond Rule. Even claimed to have written a tell-all book, but failed to get a literary agent to represent her."

"She can't have been successful," Carol observed. "I don't recall anything about the story anywhere."

"You're right, she didn't get a nibble of interest from any reputable outlet, and only a couple of quickly-forgotten mentions in the gossip columns. Maybe this was because she's a singularly unpleasant woman who, I'm told, alienates almost everyone she meets. Or perhaps a more likely explanation is related to Rule's influence in certain board rooms, where he put the word out that she wasn't to be given any opportunity to cause him trouble."

Taking another look at the woman's malevolent expression, Carol said, "I don't suppose she's traveled to the United States recently, has she?"

"Worth a look. In fact, I'll check all of them."

The deceased Fancee Porter was the sixth person on the list. Although her photograph showed her squinting into bright light, Carol could see the faint imprint of Thurmond Rule's features on her face. She was the first of the claimants Carol had seen who actually looked as if Rule blood might run in her veins.

Fancee Porter had been rootless, uncommitted. She had gained a degree in American literature at Stanford, but had never translated that achievement into anything substantial. For the next ten years, until her death, she'd led a purposeless life, never forming lasting relationships and criss-crossing the country several times, working at various low-paying jobs.

Bourke had printed out online newspaper accounts of Fancee Porter's fatal accident, as well as two graphic photos taken at the scene. "I've asked the Austin police to send a full report," said Bourke, "but it looks fair dinkum to me. She made a habit of drinking in bars, then driving home alone, or with company she'd picked up. This night she just had too much booze, lost control, slammed into some inoffensive tree and killed herself."

Next was Ian Stewart. Carol skipped through the details, having already seen his file, and turned to the final person contending for the Rule fortune. He was a child—a thin, anxious-looking boy with a scrawny neck and ears that stuck out so far Carol knew he had to be teased about them.

"Twelve-year-old Ricky Webb," said Bourke. "The list of claimants would be longer if the rest of his family hadn't got themselves killed in a boating accident. He's the sole survivor. His parents were part of a close-knit farming community in South Australia, and very active in the local church. The minister and his wife have taken Ricky into their family."

"Poor kid."

"Not so poor," said Bourke, "and the church people are quite aware of that. I'm not saying their motives aren't above board, but they have hired a hotshot legal firm to make sure Ricky gets his share of the estate."

Should the courts allocate the boy a share of the billions, Carol could imagine the adults who'd be clamoring to administer Ricky Webb's new wealth until he came of age. "I feel sorry for him," she said. "He's lost his family, and now is about to gain any number of people interested in his welfare—or more likely, the welfare of his money."

"Wouldn't that be up to Slessor, Slessor, Dunkling and Gold? I got the impression they had complete control of the Thurmond Rule estate."

"Only until the probate court rules on who gets what. And that reminds me, Mark, check if Martina Rule left a will. She can't have been anywhere as rich as daddy, but Rule did tell me when I met him that he gave his daughter anything she asked for, and I'm guessing she asked for plenty."

"My kid," said Bourke, "will be lucky if she inherits my season ticket to the Cricket Ground."

● ● ●

Deciding to escape for a few moments her constantly ringing phone, Carol redirected her calls to Bourke, left her mobile phone in her desk drawer, and came downstairs and into the embrace of a sunny afternoon. She set off for her favorite coffee shop on Oxford Street, having reached her limit as far as the tar-like liquid the Sydney Police Centre called coffee was concerned.

"Carol Ashton!" exclaimed an animated voice.

With far less enthusiasm Carol said, "Vida Drake. Is this meeting a coincidence?"

The journalist laughed. "Oh, sure. I had a psychic flash you'd be here, and bloody hell, here you are!"

Carol continued walking, and Vida Drake fell in beside her. Carol

51

sighed as she glanced at Vida. The woman was much shorter than Carol, so almost had to trot to keep up. Although her wild black hair, streaked with gray, plus her tie-dyed cotton shift and clunky sandals, gave her the appearance of a middle-aged hippie, actually she was the toughest of journalists, with the tenacity of a bulldog.

"Where are we going?" Vida inquired.

"Coffee shop."

"Oh, good. Actually, Carol, I was on my way to see you, and had braced myself to drink some of that disgusting brew you cops seem to like, but a stroll in the sun with a decent cup of coffee at the end is a much better idea."

They stopped for a *Don't Walk* sign. Resigned to Vida's company, Carol said, "I don't imagine yours was a social call. What can I do for you?"

"Know a Yank called Chuck Inman?"

"I may have heard the name."

Vida flashed her excellent teeth. "I got a *very* interesting email from Chuckie mentioning Inspector Carol Ashton several times. It seems he's got this theory . . ." She trailed off, her expectant gaze fixed on Carol's face.

It was a technique Carol had seen Vida use before. The journalist was adept at gauging from responses how much another person knew. If Vida decided the interviewee knew more than her, she would subtly troll for information; if less, Vida would try to set up a mutual trade, where she provided details in return for some advantage in access or the promise to be head of the line for breaking news.

"This American has a theory?" said Carol, offhand.

The light changed. Carol strode off the curb at an accelerated pace. Vida Drake skipped along beside her. "Thurmond Rule's estate," Vida prompted. "Money. And murder." She chortled. "Case of heir today, gone tomorrow!"

As the Commissioner had predicted, Chuck Inman was obviously courting the media. Carol said, "Don't tell me you're falling for that mind-boggling story Inman's peddling."

"It's a great story, Carol. And he's going to see me as soon as he jets in from Texas."

"An exclusive?"

Vida's nose twitched. "I wish! I hear on the grapevine he's contacted other journalists, as well as angling to get on Madeline Shipley's TV show."

"Enterprising," Carol remarked dryly.

"I've heard something else on the grapevine," said Vida in a tone indicating great significance. When Carol didn't respond, she went on, "You've looking into the suicide of a certain Rule heir."

"I am?" said Carol, inwardly fuming. This wasn't the first time something had leaked almost before it had happened. She'd had her suspicions it was someone in Superintendent Edgar's staff, but it could have come from as high as the Commissioner's office.

Although she knew Vida Drake wouldn't reveal her sources, Carol said, with the requisite amount of doubt in her voice, "And you think this is reliable information?"

"The best, so don't bother suggesting otherwise." Vida's smile was warmly ingratiating. "We're not enemies, Carol. In fact, I'd regard you as a friend."

Carol grinned in spite of herself. "I'm a friend? Not a victim of the over-zealous press?"

"Sounds good. May I quote you?"

"You may not." They'd come to the little coffee shop. Carol pushed open the door. "I'll buy you a coffee, Vida, and we'll set some ground rules. Okay?"

"Okay," said Vida, "but don't try to put anything over on me."

"As if I could—or would," said Carol virtuously. They were both aware Carol would do her best to do just that if the circumstances demanded it.

● ● ●

Carol walked back to the Police Centre alone, Vida having taken herself off to "pursue other leads." Before they parted, the journalist, gaze fixed on Carol for reactions, had confided one of the hot leads she was following concerned Eric Rule, Thurmond's long-deceased son.

"The theory is Eric's not dead," Vida had said, "and he's set on removing everyone with a claim on the estate."

Carol didn't hide her derision. "That's a ridiculous, implausible theory. Eric Rule is dead and gone. If he isn't, where's he been hiding all these years? If he's alive, why didn't he come forward the moment he heard his inheritance was up for grabs?"

Unfazed, Vida had shrugged. "Stranger things have happened," she said. "You're actively looking for someone who's popping off the Rule heirs, aren't you? One's dead in America. One's dead here. Why couldn't Eric Rule be the perp?"

"First, there's no investigation into popping off the heirs, as you put it. Second, Eric Rule is long gone, and even if he were alive, he'd have no reason to kill anyone. He'd inherit everything. Third, you really need to get yourself more accurate sources, Vida."

Now, walking in the waning sunshine, Vida's theory reminded Carol of the old black-and-white British movie, *Kind Hearts and Coronets*, she'd recently seen on late-night television. A black comedy, its plot concerned the distant heir to a dukedom, who set out to kill the ten people standing between him and the title. She recalled how amusingly each murder had been accomplished and the movie's delightfully ironic ending.

Surely the idea someone would consider eliminating the line of heirs to the Rule billions was as fanciful as the movie had been. Even so, she made a mental note to have Mark Bourke check the boating accident that had killed Ricky Webb's family.

At least one of Ricky's parents, she realized, would have a closer relationship to Thurmond Rule than Ricky himself. And perhaps elimination of that person had suddenly brought the present heirs into contention.

Back in her office, she found several voice mail messages waiting for her. Leota's was succinct. "Carol, I'm leaving for Canberra right now. The usual security flap. I'll move heaven and earth to be back in Sydney for the weekend. Love you."

Today was Wednesday. Two days before Leota would be pressing her for at least some idea of whether Carol would consider joining her in America. Carol couldn't help feeling relieved to have more time before making any decisions. Of course, with the pressures of this new investigation, time to do anything else was limited.

Carol grinned wryly to herself. She'd just have to shove the whole problem down to her subconscious and let it do the decision-making for her. "I hope the hell you know what to do," she told it, "because I sure don't."

CHAPTER SIX

"I would have said Ian was the last person on earth to kill himself, but . . ." Gaye Mason, a faded woman with a careworn face, made a helpless gesture. She looked around the room, as though hoping for some answer to be found in its plain furnishings.

A slight jerk of the head from Carol directed Anne Newsome to continue the interview. Anne, her voice warmly sympathetic, said, "This is a very sad time for you, but we'd appreciate it if you'd answer a few questions."

When Gaye Mason nodded assent, Anne asked, "Did your brother-in-law ever mention suicide?"

This was a good question. Many people intending to kill themselves would bring up the subject of suicide, however obliquely, in the weeks or days before they acted.

"No, never, dearie. Not once. I'd've remembered something like that. I'm not saying Ian didn't get a bit down in the mouth at times—we all do, don't we—but as for killing himself, I don't believe the idea ever crossed his mind."

Shaking her head, Anne said, "It must have been a terrible shock."

"Dearie, you can have no idea! I never would have gone out for the day if I'd had the slightest thought . . ." Her eyes filled with tears.

"We've been wondering where he could have obtained the Valium he took," said Anne in a confiding tone. "Would you have any thoughts?"

A fleeting expression of outrage flashed across Gaye Mason's face. "You know, it might sound funny, but I can hardly forgive Ian for that! I won't have drugs in the house, not even aspirin, and he knew that very well. As for where he might have got the tablets, I've no idea. Ian's hardly seen the inside of a doctor's office these last ten years. He was that healthy, see?" She gave a sudden sob and tears spilled down her cheeks. "And yet he went and killed himself."

After waiting for Gaye Mason to dab at her wet face with a tissue, Anne said, "Your brother-in-law was distantly related to Thurmond Rule."

"So he told me. Ian has a copy of the family tree someone sent him. Showed me where he was on it. Second cousin removed a few times, I think he said. It was too complicated for me, so I took his word for it." She looked down at her hands twisted in her lap. "All that money—what's it worth to Ian now?"

"Was he excited about the possibility of inheriting a lot of money?"

"Ian wasn't one to cross his bridges before he came to them. He was pleased, of course, but he said he'd only really believe it when he had the cash in his hands."

57

Carol interposed to say, "Did Ian speak to anyone else who's also making a claim on the Rule estate?"

"Now that you mention it, there was someone. Came here to see Ian a couple of weeks ago. Don't recall his last name, but he called himself Kent. Works for Qantas as a steward, or flight attendant, or whatever they call them these days."

"Would his last name have been Humphries?" Carol asked.

"That's it! Kent Humphries. The bloke had this idea the lawyer firm that's handling everything might not be on the up and up. He wanted everyone to stick together, and not let the lawyers take most of the money, like they do if given half a chance."

"And what did Ian think of this?"

"Well, he could see it might be a good idea, but he wondered if this Kent bloke was really just sounding him out to see if Ian had a proper claim. Don't know if Ian saw him again, but I think they spoke on the phone."

Anne asked a few more questions about Ian Stewart's friendship with John Hansen, the man who had found the body. Gaye Mason was close to effusive, describing how nice Hansen had been, and how he'd helped with the funeral arrangements. "He lives nearby, and every day or so Ian would go there, or John would come here. Best friends for years. Liked their sport, they did. And played a lot of chess. Never understood the game myself, but they'd spend hours bent over the board."

After checking the time, Carol brought the interview to a close. She and Anne had also arranged to see Hansen before he left for work.

John Hansen lived in a dingy little block of flats in Leichhardt. The rumble of heavy traffic on Parramatta Road provided a constant background noise. Hansen opened his front door slowly, peering suspiciously at them. Carol introduced herself and Anne Newsome, and reminded him they had made an appointment to see him.

"Oh, yeah. Come in."

He was a skinny man with stooped shoulders and a faintly defeated air. He led them through to a small, tidy room filled with ancient furniture and the smell of pipe tobacco. Waving them to sit on a bumpy settee, he said, "Been friends with Ian for forty years. Went to school together. Even when Doreen died, he soldiered on. I'll never believe he killed himself."

"So what do you think happened?" Carol asked.

"Jesus, I don't know. Maybe he suddenly lost his marbles. Maybe it was some sort of silly joke that went wrong." He glanced at Anne, got rather red, and finally said, "When I found him there on the bed, for a moment I thought . . ."

"What did you think, Mr. Hansen?"

"Well . . . maybe Ian was doing something . . . sexual."

"Auto-eroticism?" Carol suggested.

"Whatever funny name you like to use—jerking yourself off is what I call it." He cleared his throat. "When I looked closer, I saw it couldn't be that. It was like Ian was sleeping, except for the plastic bag around his head."

"If it isn't suicide, or an accident, that leaves murder."

"Murder?" Carol's use of the word clearly jolted him. "No one would want to murder Ian. He had no enemies. Quiet bloke. In all the years I've known him, never seen him pick an argument with anyone."

"He told you about the inheritance?"

Hansen was scornful. "Pie in the sky. Never happen."

Responding to a glance from Carol, Anne said, "Did you know another claimant to the Rule fortune had contacted Ian?"

"Yeah, he told me. Qantas guy. Don't remember his name, but he was a steward, or whatever you call them. I reckoned he'd be a bit of a poofter, but Ian said not."

"Do you know what they discussed?"

"Yeah. The bloke wanted Ian to join with him and the others to gang up against the lawyers. Said otherwise they'd pull a fast one."

"And did he agree to join with them?" Anne asked.

"No, not Ian. He always thought the best of people, you see." A slight smile twitched his lips. "Even thought lawyers were okay. That's how he was."

Hansen had no idea where Stewart had obtained the Valium. "Myself, I wouldn't touch the stuff. Women's pills," he said scornfully. Asked about the suicide note, a shadow of pain showed on his face. "You know," he said, "I thought Ian would have at least mentioned my name. Said goodbye. I would've, if it had been me." He shook his head. "Jesus, we've been mates forever."

● ● ●

Carol had made a ten o'clock appointment to see Hector and Juanita Paz. Ambrose Slessor's call had obviously smoothed the way, as the single guard at the entrance immediately opened the looming gates to the estate and waved them through when Carol said who she was. "Drive down to the house. Mr. Ledmark will be waiting for you."

As she negotiated the curving driveway she'd walked down last time, she said to Anne, "Mark and I met Ledmark when we came to see Thurmond Rule after his daughter died. Unlike the other security guards, he appeared to have a sense of humor, so you should find it easy to get him chatting about Rule's daughter."

Although Martina Rule had had the entire top floor of a luxury block overlooking Double Bay, she'd often stayed at her father's mansion. Carol had discussed with Anne the areas she wanted her to deal with when she questioned Ledmark, reminding her to cover a fascinating fact Bourke had discovered—Martina's will had named Juanita Paz as the major beneficiary, but then, abruptly, Martina had made a new will, cutting Juanita out.

As they drew up to the front of the stolid sandstone edifice, David Ledmark stepped forward. As previously, he was wearing a dark gray uniform, but this time had no name badge. "Inspector Ashton," he said warmly as she and Anne got out of the car. "How nice to see you again."

60

Carol introduced Anne Newsome. "Mr. Ledmark, I would appreciate it if you'd answer a few questions for Constable Newsome while I'm speaking with Mr. Paz and his wife."

He gave Anne's trim figure an appreciative glance. "I'd be delighted."

They followed him into the house. "It's a bit like looking after a mothballed museum," he remarked as he led them past the open doors of rooms containing furniture draped with white dustcovers. Seeing Anne peering at the unmistakable outline of a grand piano, he added, "The doors are kept open to maintain the same temperature and humidity throughout."

"Looks a little like the set of a horror film."

Ledmark grinned at Carol's comment. "The horror is the stuff in this place, Inspector. I shouldn't speak ill of the dead, but Mr. Rule had the most excruciatingly bad taste as far as décor is concerned. It beats me how things that cost so much can be so ugly."

He opened the door of the same unattractively furnished room Carol had seen on her first visit. The furniture here was uncovered, and demonstrated clearly the truth of Ledmark's critical comments.

"If you wait here, Constable Newsome, I'll take Inspector Ashton to Mr. Paz, and then come back for your"—he broke off to grin at Anne—"searching interrogation."

"How long were you with Mr. Rule?" Carol asked him as they continued down the hallway.

"About the same as Hector Paz, I'd say. That'd make it around ten years, give or take a month or so."

"Mr. Slessor mentioned you'd acted as Mr. Rule's personal body-guard."

"I rose through the ranks," Ledmark said with a smile. "Started off manning the gate at night, and worked my way up to bodyguard. Mr. Rule sent me off for all the training necessary, so I was pretty well prepared for anything; however, in the years I guarded him, the worst I had to do was strong-arm a few people who wanted to get too close. His daughter was a lot more challenging."

"You were Martina Rule's bodyguard too?"

"On occasions." He made a face. "She was a handful. Went looking for trouble, and often found it."

Opening a door, he stood aside for Carol to enter. It was a small sitting room, flooded with light from the garden outside the tall windows. Unlike the rest of the house, the furniture was sleekly contemporary.

"Our own little area," said Paz with a smooth smile. He was as snappily dressed as the first time Carol had seen him, but his wife was wearing faded jeans and a T-shirt instead of the crisp green nurse's uniform.

"Inspector," she said in her soft voice, "I've coffee here, ready for you. Or would you prefer tea?"

"Coffee would be fine. Thank you."

Carol sat in the proffered chair, thinking how, with similar dark hair and eyes, Hector and Juanita Paz could almost be brother and sister. And they spoke the same excellent English with the same beguiling accent.

"We're wondering how we can help you, Inspector," said Paz, sitting with feline grace on a chair adjacent to Carol's. "Of course we'll answer whatever you care to ask, but I wonder if I could inquire what exactly it is you're looking for."

Knowing Ambrose Slessor had almost certainly filled Paz in about the reason for her visit, Carol said blandly, "Just filling in a few gaps, Mr. Paz. We're investigating another matter, and as it indirectly concerns Mr. Rule, it's necessary to check a few details."

Juanita Paz bit her lip. Perched uneasily on the edge of her chair, she said, "We're not in any trouble, are we?"

"Not at all. I just have a few routine questions." Carol almost smiled as she mouthed this hoary police cliché.

"Do you really need Juanita here?" asked Hector Paz. "I can cover anything you need to know."

His wife's face reflected the hope she might escape Carol's questioning. "Hector knows more about everything than I do."

"Actually, Ms. Paz, it's you I need to see."

"Oh? Me?" She clasped her hands. "Is it about Mr. Rule? My nursing? Dr. McMinn can tell you everything concerning the treatment. I followed his instructions exactly."

"I've spoken to Dr. McMinn."

This information didn't allay Juanita Paz's anxiety. Her hands fluttered, and she seemed about to speak, when her husband broke in with, "My wife is very nervous about the police. Please don't take this personally, Inspector Ashton, but in Colombia . . . Let's just say the members of law enforcement are not as trusted as they are here."

Carol said, "I understand. Please don't be alarmed, Ms. Paz. I just have a few things to clear up."

"Of course I'll help in any way I can."

Carol took her through the regimen of medications used in the last days of Rule's life. Clearly this wasn't too threatening an area, as Juanita Paz relaxed as she confirmed the details Dr. McMinn had given Carol on the phone.

When this subject appeared effectively covered, Hector Paz said, "More coffee, Inspector, before you go?"

Not so fast, thought Carol, amused at his obvious desire to get her out the door. "There is one other matter."

He paused in the action of getting up. Sinking back in his chair, he said, "Yes?" with just a hint of arrogant impatience.

Carol directed her whole attention at his wife. "Martina Rule's will named you, Juanita Paz, as principal heir. And then she suddenly made a new will, not long before she died, this time leaving you out. What was your reaction to that?"

There had been little cash in the daughter's estate, as Martina Rule appeared to have spent the money her father gave to her fast as she received it. Her possessions, however—jewelry, fine furniture and other costly goods—had been valued conservatively at three hundred thousand dollars.

Hector Paz was on his feet, swollen with righteous anger. "What are you implying? Martina was extremely grateful for the wonderful care my wife gave to her father, and on an impulse, named Juanita in her will. It was, of course, far too generous of her. Upon reflection, Martina changed her will. We understood completely."

Carol said, "I'm puzzled as to why Martina Rule would name your wife in her will in the first place, given that Martina was a young woman who could hardly have expected to die so soon. Surely she could show her appreciation with a valuable gift of some sort, rather than promises of something much later."

Juanita Paz put her hands over her face and gave a sob. "What am I supposed to have done wrong? I didn't ask for anything to be given to me. I didn't expect anything."

"You've upset my wife," said Hector Paz with cold dignity. "I'd like you to go now."

• • •

In the car on the way back to the Police Centre, Carol and Anne exchanged accounts. Anne raised her eyebrows at Carol's description of Juanita Paz's reaction to questioning. "Really? That's not the Juanita that Dave Ledmark described to me. He said she was a bit of a free spirit and game for anything. That's why she and Martina got on so well."

"*Dave* Ledmark, is it?"

Anne grinned. "You did tell me to chat him up. He's a nice guy. I'd tend to believe him when he says Juanita and Martina acted like close friends, sharing confidences."

Carol chuckled. "I imagine Martina's confidences could get pretty raunchy."

"Dave did say he got the impression nothing Martina did could ever throw Juanita."

"Did he know about the will, that was later changed?"

"He said he wasn't surprised. Juanita had Martina wound around her little finger most of the time, but Martina blew hot and cold. She'd love you one day, and hate you the next."

64

This picture was so much at odds with the impression Juanita Paz had made on Carol that she said, "We could be talking about two different people."

"You did say she was scared of the police. Who knows what happened to her in Colombia before she came to Australia?"

"You're right, Anne, of course. It could be a knee-jerk response to authority. And that would explain why Hector Paz was so protective."

"Dave Ledmark doesn't like Paz at all. Says he's Teflon-coated. Nothing's ever his fault."

Parking the car, Carol said, "You speak so enthusiastically about David Ledmark, I'm wondering if you intend to see him again."

Anne reddened a little. "He did ask me out, but if he's involved some way in the investigation, of course I can't accept."

Bourke met Carol and Anne as they came up the stairs. Laughing, he put up his hand. "Stop right there, Carol. You've got a visitor, and you're going to need back-up. No way are you seeing her alone."

"Who is it?"

"One Ophelia Rule, born Susan Jordan. She caused quite a scene downstairs when told you weren't in, and even more of a scene when it was tactfully suggested she might make an appointment to see you. My attempts to pour oil on troubled waters nearly got my head knocked off."

Amused at this picture, Carol asked, "Where is she now? A cell?"

"I've got Maureen babysitting her in your office. We didn't think it safe to leave the woman unsupervised. In a split second she'd be rifling through your desk."

When Carol and Bourke entered, Maureen Oatland's face was full of suppressed amusement. Getting to her feet, she said, she said, "Ms. Rule, may I present Detective Inspector Ashton."

The photograph of Susan Jordan/Ophelia Rule had not depicted an attractive woman. In the flesh she was even more strikingly ugly. It was not because of her commonplace features or thickset body. Bitter, spiteful hostility emanated from her so palpably that Carol could almost see it as a dark cloud filling the room.

"You!" the woman said, stabbing a thick forefinger in Carol's direction. "You've got to stop them."

Carol gestured to Maureen she could leave. Obviously enjoying the show, Maureen mouthed "Must I?" with her back to the visitor. After she'd reluctantly departed, Bourke took her vacated seat and Carol slid behind the security of her desk before saying, "Good morning, Ms. Rule."

"Don't good morning me. I'm bloody here to get justice."

"In what way?"

She hitched her chair closer to the desk and leaned forward. "Those bastard lawyers are milking my estate. I want an accounting. I want them prosecuted."

"You're referring to Slessor, Slessor, Dunkling and Gold, I presume," said Carol, letting the names roll off her tongue.

"That's them. Weasely bastards. Got their mates in the courts to put them in charge of the whole shebang, so they can loot the estate with impunity. Pigs at the trough." She glared at Carol, then at Bourke. "I want it stopped. It's my inheritance."

"Very understandable you'd be concerned," said Bourke with a perfectly straight face. "And you'd be worried about your brother's share, too."

Evidently reading some derogatory meaning into Bourke's comment, she snarled, "My brother Nick's a bloody vegetable, hooked to bloody machines. I've got power of attorney. Okay? It's all perfectly legal." Her demeanor dared him to disagree.

Carol uncapped her pen, "Do you have specific evidence of wrong-doing?"

"Evidence? How could I have evidence? You think they're stupid enough to give themselves away? They might be bastards, but they're not dumb."

Carol re-capped her pen. "Ms. Rule, I'm sorry, but accusations without any evidence at all of wrong-doing make it very difficult for me to do anything." She leaned back in her chair, careful not to catch Bourke's eye, and added, "I'm afraid my hands are tied."

The stream of invective Ophelia Rule spewed out caused Carol to blink—not at the words, but at the astonishing venom with which they were delivered.

When she'd run out of steam, Carol said, "Since you're here, Ms. Rule, I wonder if you'd answer a few questions."

This request was met with heavy suspicion. "What about?"

"About the whole issue of the Rule estate."

Ophelia narrowed her eyes. "Might it help get those bastard lawyers?"

"It's possible," said Carol smoothly, ignoring the sound Bourke made, which sounded suspiciously like a chuckle disguised as a cough. "The more information I have . . . Well, who knows where it may lead?"

After a pause, Ophelia said, "All right. What do you want to know?"

"Have you talked with any of the other heirs?"

Ophelia jittered her fingernails against the edge of the desk, a sound Carol found intensely annoying. After considering Carol's question at length, she finally replied, "What if I have?"

"Did anyone suggest to you that Mr. Rule's solicitors might be untrustworthy?"

"You don't think I'm smart enough to work it out on my own? Is that it?"

Argumentative was too mild a description, Carol decided. This woman was confrontational, belligerent and spoiling for an out-and-out fight.

"Ms. Rule, these questions are designed to clarify the situation, and are not in any way a personal attack on you."

Carol's mild tone was apparently convincing, as Ophelia sat back in her chair with a grunt. "Kent Humphries started the ball rolling," she said. "Really put the wind up me. I think he warned everyone about the bloody lawyers, except for that little kid in South Australia."

"Even in America?"

"Chuck?" Amazingly, Ophelia Rule's expression had softened a little. "Oh, yes, Humphries went and saw Chuck in Houston. Don't know about the other one with the stupid name. *Fancee*—can you imagine?"

"Fancee Porter was killed in a car accident a few days ago," said Bourke.

"Yeah, I know." There was a tinge of satisfaction in her tone. "Chuck called me."

"Did he mention—"

"That someone bumped her off? Yeah, but that's Chuck. He's into conspiracies." She sounded almost indulgent. "Shit stupid, if you ask me," she went on. "I mean, if one of us is killing the others, whoever's left at the end has to be the one, right? *So* dumb!"

"Summed up perfectly," said Bourke, sounding impressed.

When Ophelia looked pleased with the compliment, Bourke took advantage of her momentary flash of good humor to ask, "How did you find out you were a blood relative? You knew long before the hunt started for heirs."

"Got the diagram of the Rule family tree in the mail early last year. Huge sheet of paper. Took up half the dining room table. My name had a red circle around it. Took it quick smart to an expert, and he said it was rinky-dink. I was a Rule, no worries." Her face darkened. "Of course that old son-of-a-bitch, Thurmond Rule, refused to the end to admit I was his relative. Hope he burns in hell!"

"You have no idea who sent the family tree to you?" Carol asked. Stewart, she recalled, had received one too. She made a mental note to check if any of the other heirs had a similar mystery mailing.

Ophelia's heavy cheeks trembled as she shook her head. "Not a clue who sent it, and don't care."

"Did you notice the postmark?"

Ophelia prickled at an insult only she saw. "Are you saying I'm too dim to look at the envelope?"

Carol resisted rolling her eyes. "Of course not, Ms. Rule, but many people don't think of it."

"Well, *I* did. Mailed in Sydney. No return address. And before you ask, I didn't keep the envelope. No reason to."

"Have you been out of the country recently?" said Bourke.

Impatient irritation flooding her face, Ophelia Rule snapped, "You've got a way with stupid questions, you know that? Oz is good enough for me. And why would I be gadding about when I've got all this money coming to me, eh? Answer me that."

She hauled herself to her feet. "I'm not answering any more questions, but I've got one of my own." She glared at Carol. "What I want to know is, are you going to follow up on my complaint or not?"

Carol said, "I intend to see Mr. Slessor at the earliest opportunity."

"So why didn't you say so to begin with?" A final glower, and she stalked out the door.

"Escort her out of the building, Mark," said Carol. "And make damn sure she doesn't double back."

● ● ●

After lunch Superintendent Edgar called in to see Carol. "I've put Lester Upton on your team," he said with the air of an exceptionally generous benefactor. He paused, evidently awaiting her enthusiastic response.

Carol, who'd hoped for the addition of at least two experienced officers, forced herself to thank him with appropriate gratitude. She didn't know Les Upton well, but assessed him as a reliable, plodding officer who lacked both initiative and insight. In his favor, Upton appeared to be dependable and hard-working, and could be trusted to pursue any task given to him with tenacity, if not with flair.

"I'm sending Mark Bourke to South Australia tomorrow morning to have a close look at the accident that killed Ricky Webb's parents and baby sister," she said. "He'll be away two days."

Normally such an announcement would provoke her superior into a flurry of questions about the cost benefits of such an expenditure on travel and accommodation, but the Commissioner's stamp of approval on the investigation had done away with such carping. "Excellent," said Edgar. "Keep me informed. Fully informed."

Les Upton turned up in Carol's office half an hour later. Looking at his regular features and neat, spare body, Carol decided he was one of those men she would judge handsome, if only his face had been animated and his body language had shown some energy and enthusiasm. Instead, his good looks were dulled by his stolid, passive manner.

"I was told to report to you," he said in a monotone.

Determined to accentuate the positive, Carol said, "I'm pleased to have you join the team, Les. We need your zeal."

"My zeal?" He seemed mildly astonished at the word.

"In checking facts, running down details."

Upton gave a slight smile. "Oh, *that* zeal."

Pleasantly surprised that Upton appeared to have a sense of humor, Carol said, "Martina Rule, as you no doubt know, was hit by a vehicle in a suburban mall's parking lot and killed. The initial investigation pointed to an accident; however, later information suggests we should look at her death more closely. That's where you come in."

They went through the file together, establishing the areas Upton would concentrate upon, then he left to find a vacant desk and establish his base.

Bourke had given Carol the name and number of Martina Rule's solicitor, Seymour Burton. Carol expected some opposition to her questions, but when she called the lawyer was ebulliently cooperative. "I don't mind telling you, Inspector, Martina Rule was quite a challenge as a client. Impulsive is the word I'd use. She changed her will on a whim many times, and a simple codicil would never do it. No, she always demanded an entirely new document."

"So it wasn't a surprise when she disinherited Juanita Paz?"

"Oh, good heavens, no! Martina was quite inclined to name in her will her best friend of the moment. A few weeks or months later,

70

the person would be out of favor, and consequently no longer a beneficiary. Her final will, current when she died, was unusual for her, as it benefited several different animal welfare organizations."

"Did she say why she was naming these organizations?"

"I didn't ask," said Burton with a laugh, "but it would have been the same reason as usual—someone had fallen out of favor."

"And this someone would have been Juanita Paz. Did you ever have any conversations with Martina Rule about her?"

"In a way," said Burton. "Martina brought Ms. Paz in with her when she instructed me to draw up yet another will, this time naming Juanita Paz."

"How did Juanita Paz strike you at this meeting? Did she seem elated to be named in the will?"

"As I recall, she was very calm. I'd say subdued. She did laugh at all of Martina's jokes—which were never particularly funny." He chuckled. "But if Martina had named me in her will, I'd have laughed at them too."

Carol thanked the lawyer for his help, and rang off. She still had her hand on the receiver, intending to call her aunt to say she'd be late home and not to wait dinner, when the phone rang beneath her fingers.

"Hi, Carol. This is Yancey. Yancey Blake."

Sybil's lover. Carol had only spoken to her briefly on a couple of other occasions. "Is this about Aunt Sarah's portrait and the cocktail party? I'm sorry, I don't—"

"Not the cocktail party. Look, Carol, no doubt as usual you're super busy, but I'm down your end of town, and I'd appreciate it if you could leave the office and see me for a few minutes."

"Unfortunately I'm—"

"Please."

Irritated Yancey Blake had no compunction in interrupting her, Carol was about to brush the artist off when Yancey said, "It's about Sybil."

Carol felt a rush of sudden concern. A picture of Sybil leapt into

71

her mind—her red hair gleaming in sunshine, her lips curving in a smile. "Is she okay? Has something happened?"

"She's fine."

"Then what's this about, Yancey? Stop the mystery routine, and tell me."

"I'll tell you when we meet."

"This isn't a good—"

"It's important. Is there somewhere near the Police Centre we can meet? It'll only take a few minutes."

The woman was inexorable. Carol gave directions to the coffee shop where she'd gone with Vida the day before. "See you there in twenty minutes, Yancey. And I'll be pushed for time, so keep it short."

A brisk walk in the sun restored Carol's equanimity, so she greeted Yancey Blake graciously when they met inside the coffee shop. Sitting down at one of the small tables crowding the limited space, Carol said, "Forgive me if I was abrupt on the phone."

Yancey had an engaging smile. "Forgive me if I was pushy."

Of medium height, she had a generous figure, brown hair and eyes and a singularly penetrating gaze. Maybe, Carol thought, that came with being a portrait painter.

"You're a bit of a disappointment to me," Carol said. "I expect a genuine artist to have oil paint under her fingernails, and perhaps an artistic smear on one cheek."

"I'm equally disappointed, Carol. Blonde, striking . . . Doesn't go with the image of a tough cop."

They ordered coffee. Carol leaned back. "So much for chitchat. Why did you want to see me?"

"Sybil and I are . . . parting. It's not that I don't love her. I do, very much."

"This is nothing to do with me."

Yancey gave a short laugh. "It's everything to do with you." When Carol frowned, Yancey went on, "I'm not trying to be mysterious. First, let me tell you Sybil has no idea I'm meeting you today.

If she knew, she'd wonder why, because unless you were commissioning me to paint your portrait, there's no way I'd be talking with you. We have absolutely nothing in common. Except Sybil."

Carol let her breath out in an impatient sigh. "What are you saying?"

"I'm saying she never got over you. I'm saying you're the third person in our bed. I'm saying for Sybil anyone who isn't you, is second-best."

Astonished, Carol stared at her. "That just isn't true. Ask her, she'll tell you. We can barely be friends."

"Oh, I have asked her. And Sybil denies it—and believes she's telling the truth."

"But you know better."

For a moment the sting of pain showed on Yancey Blake's face. "Yes, I know better. That's why I'm leaving her."

In her pocket, Carol's phone chirruped. She excused herself, and took the call.

"Carol?" It was Bourke. "You're not going to believe this, but you know Jim Flint, the guy from Western Australia? He's dead."

CHAPTER SEVEN

"So I was like, yeah, why don't you go drinking without me? I just love being stuck in this dump with your shitty step-sister and her whiney kids." The young woman's thin lips twisted in a sneer. "And Jim was, like, stop nagging me, you bitch. Know what I mean?"

In her late teens, Jim Flint's girlfriend, Kirra, was pretty in a pinched-face sort of way. Her miniscule skirt and midriff-baring top made it clear there was no spare flesh on her near-anorexic frame. Nor, it appeared, did she have any spare grief for her murdered boyfriend.

Carol asked, "What time was this?"

"Jeez, I dunno. 'Bout six? Deb'll know." Over her shoulder she screeched, "Deb? What time did Jim go out last night?"

"How the fuck would I know?" was shouted from the back of the house.

Kirra put her hands on her hips. "Well, six'll have to do you then, won't it?"

Carol and Maureen Oatland exchanged amused glances. As Mark Bourke was on his way to South Australia, Carol had taken Maureen with her this Friday morning.

Carol said, "Jim usually met his friends at the pub? Is that right?"

"I suppose." She shook a cigarette out of a crumpled pack, struck a match, inhaled a long draw of smoke. Exhaling a gray stream in their direction, she said, "And don't ask me about his drinking mates. Don't know any of 'em."

"Anyone ever pick him up here?" Maureen asked.

"Nah. Jim always took his truck to the pub. Didn't like anyone else driving." Her thin nose wrinkled in disgust. "Silly bugger wouldn't even let me get behind the wheel even once, all that way over from Perth. Shit boring just sitting there hour after hour, know what I mean?"

The truck in question had been parked in a dead-end street adjacent to an abandoned industrial site near Sydney Airport about six kilometers from the hotel where Flint had been drinking. Jim Flint was in the vehicle, slumped over the wheel, very dead. Blood from his cut throat had pooled in his lap and dribbled down his legs to coagulate at his feet.

To spare his stepsister's feelings when she identified the body earlier that day, Flint's face had been washed to remove the splashes of blood that had spurted from his carotid artery, and an opaque plastic sheet had been pulled up to conceal the gaping wound in his throat.

Such niceties appeared unnecessary. Deb Rowland had taken a cursory glance at the corpse, said, "Yeah, it's Jim, the stupid bastard," and marched out of the viewing room.

It was clear that neither his stepsister nor his girlfriend was devastated by Jim Flint's violent death. After leaving the house Maureen said, "So much for mourning, eh? Never seen drier eyes. Not even a pretense at tears. Doesn't it make you wonder why either of them would put up with the guy? Hell, you'd think the girlfriend could do better."

"Kirra's a bit of a tough case, herself."

"Ah, yes, Carol, but not bad looking. That's enough for a lot of males, you know." She gave a hoot of laughter. "Must be why I'm so successful!"

Carol had to smile. Maureen had alarmed several of her workmates with her earthy attitude. Large in every way, and imbued with a lusty appetite for both food and, reportedly, sex, she had a predatory gaze that seemed to both attract and unsettle the men with whom she worked, particularly the younger ones.

Flint's chosen watering hole, *The Quitters' Arms*, was a seedy suburban pub with a décor that included cracked wall tiles and a floor sticky with spilled drinks.

"Jim? Well, yeah," said the barmaid, disconcertingly young and fresh-faced, "I know the guy well enough to never get on the wrong side of him. Last night? He was here. Why, what's up?"

"He's met with a bit of an accident," said Maureen with a wolfish grin. "Are you sure he was in the bar last night?"

"Place was packed to the rafters, but Jim always makes an impression. He's got a loud voice, and doesn't mind using it."

"Drink much, did he?"

"Always."

"Did you notice when he left, and if he was with anyone?"

"I was run off my feet, so I didn't see him go. Think it was latish, though. As for anyone with him . . ." She shrugged.

Carol had deliberately asked Maureen to lead the questioning, as she seemed so much more at home in this environment than Carol. Watching the interview proceed, she was amused to notice in appearance Maureen looked far closer to the stereotype of golden-hearted barmaid than the interviewee herself did.

"So Jim doesn't drink with the same crowd every time?" Maureen was saying.

"He pals up with whoever's here. Jim's prickly, if you know what I mean, and lately he's got up the nose of a few of the regulars, so he's not too popular. Not that it seems to worry him."

"Got into fights, did he?" Maureen inquired.

"More shoving matches. Jim might have a short fuse, but he picks his mark. Always careful not to pick on someone bigger and meaner."

"Anyone in particular that's got it in for him?"

The barmaid laughed. "Join the queue," she said.

Maureen arranged to come back in the evening when the regular patrons would be available for questioning. She would liaise with the local police, who were conducting a door-to-door in the area adjacent to the pub, asking if anyone had noticed Flint or his truck on Thursday evening.

Before returning to the Centre, Carol and Maureen called in to view Flint's vehicle, which had been towed away for forensic examination after Liz's scene-of-crime team had finished work and the body had been removed.

The truck had obviously been Jim Flint's pride and joy. Bright red and highly polished, it had a souped-up engine, huge tires, and many chrome enhancements. The two custom-made leather bucket seats were special order, as was the leather-covered steering wheel.

"The way I see it," said the forensic technician in charge of the examination, "the victim was definitely killed in the vehicle. He's sitting here behind the wheel drinking whiskey straight out of the bottle, not suspecting a thing. Someone slashes his throat. From the way the blood spurts, the victim's sitting front and center, not turned to face whoever killed him."

"He could be asleep, or drunk," Carol said.

"Drunk or not, you'd think he'd wake up quick smart when he was attacked." He pointed to the floor of the cabin. "This bloke tarted up the truck with non-standard mats—high quality thick carpeting. When we took out the mat on the driver's side, it was saturated with blood, but not scuffed, or twisted about like it would have, if there'd been a struggle. He didn't thrash around, he just died."

Carol peered into the cabin. Blood was everywhere: on the steering wheel, dried in a V-shaped stain on the driver's seat, splashed on the dashboard. "You're thinking someone in the passenger seat killed him?"

"Two scenarios. One, there's a passenger, and he leans over and slices the victim's throat. As the steering wheel's on the right side of the cabin, it'd help if the killer was left-handed. Whatever, it'd be a bit awkward, but not impossible, particularly if there's no resistance. Alternatively, the perp's outside. He opens the driver's door, and gets to the victim that way. The post mortem will establish the direction of the cut, which should settle the modus operandi."

"Messy way to kill someone," said Maureen.

He nodded agreement. "Personally, I wouldn't choose it. Someone's been very careful. You'd think blood had to have got on the killer, but we haven't found any handprints, gloved or not. No smears of blood on the door handles, or anywhere else you'd expect the perp would touch."

As they drove away from the vehicle facility, Carol said, "It seems Flint leaves the pub and drives six kilometers to park in a darkened dead-end street. What's that tell you?"

"Female company," said Maureen. "He's parking for a quick blow-job. Or perhaps it could be a drug deal gone wrong."

"The cut throat doesn't look like a drug deal to me. And if it were drugs, a simple stabbing would be more likely. This is too elaborate a set-up."

Maureen said, "Jim Flint strikes me as the sort of guy who'd end up being bashed to death by someone bigger and nastier. It's hard to imagine him sitting meekly in his truck while someone slits his throat. Maybe the post mortem will tell us why he didn't put up a fight."

Carol was hoping Leota would be up from Canberra on Saturday morning, so she said, "Maureen, I've a big favor to ask. The Commissioner's clout got Flint's post mortem scheduled at ten tomorrow. I know it's Saturday, but could you attend in my place?"

"Jeff Duke doing the slicing and dicing?" When Carol nodded, Maureen chuckled. "I'll be there," she said. "I've always rather fancied Jeff."

● ● ●

Kent Humphries had been out of the country for the past week. He'd been one of the cabin crew on a Qantas flight returning to Sydney from Los Angeles Thursday. Carol had arranged to meet him at his Bondi flat on Friday afternoon. She went alone, as Maureen was seeing Liz Carey for a preliminary report on the Flint crime scene.

She was early for the appointment, so Carol made a detour to drive along Campbell Parade, which ran the length of Bondi beach, famous in tourist guides as *the* beach to see in Sydney. Carol didn't agree, believing Sydney's northern beaches were far superior. Even so, she had to admit Bondi looked spectacular today, with white breakers rolling majestically to break on the perfect curve of pale sand. Although it was a weekday, the beach held a scattering of bright umbrellas, and Campbell Parade was crowded with people, eating ice creams, skylarking, or simply taking in the sights.

With reluctance Carol steered the car away from the sparkling water, the shrieks of seagulls, and the clean, salty air. Tranquility always touched her when she contemplated the ocean. Perhaps she should live, as Sybil did, overlooking a beautiful beach. Her own home had a view of the still waters of Middle Harbour, but there was something about the restless sea that spoke to her.

An image of Sybil's house, the steep front steps, Sybil, smiling, turning to look down at her, popped into Carol's head. She resolutely shoved it away, turning her thoughts to the matter at hand.

Mark Bourke had checked when Kent Humphries had been rostered to fly as a member of a Qantas cabin crew. Looking at the dates of Martina Rule, and Ian Stewart's deaths, it appeared Humphries had been in Sydney on both occasions. This could be entirely coincidental, but it was tantalizing, especially considering the fact Humphries had also had several days off in Los Angeles around the time of Fancee Porter's accident. Information on internal flights to ascertain if Humphries had flown to Texas during this period was not yet available.

Carol climbed red terra-cotta steps to the front top floor apartment. She paused to look at the view. Neither beach nor headlands could be seen from this vantage point, but the meeting of the two distinct blues of sky and sea was beautiful enough.

The door opened behind her. "Inspector Ashton. You're very punctual. Come in." His voice had the lightest of Scottish accents.

She had been drawn to the photograph of Kent Humphries because of the humor she'd detected in his subtly unbalanced face. Now, seeing him in actuality, Carol found this asymmetrical cast to his features rather disconcerting. The eyebrow set higher than its fellow gave him a constant quizzical look, and his crooked mouth seemed dragged down at one corner in a self-deprecating moue.

Seating Carol where she could look out at the distant ocean, he said, "Refreshments, Inspector? As a flight attendant, I guarantee to serve them with panache."

"Thank you, no. I just have a few questions, Mr. Humphries."

Amiable, he sat down opposite her. "Fire away. I'll answer them as if plugged into a lie detector." His flippant tone was relaxed, as if there could be no issue Carol could raise that could cause him a moment's concern.

"Have you ever met Fancee Porter?"

"Oh, God, yes. Had a stopover in LA and hopped a flight to Austin to see her."

Hiding her surprise at how easily this revelation had been obtained, Carol asked why he'd decided to visit Fancee Porter.

Evidently the opportunity to answer this question was welcome. With a smile, he settled back comfortably, and began, "Well first off, as you know, I'm one of the heirs to the Rule fortune."

"How did you find out you were in line to inherit?"

"I always knew I was related to them one way or other. I remember mum telling me all about Thurmond Rule when I was a kid. She had this fantasy he'd turn up one day with hands full of dollars, and everything'd be all right. Never happened, of course."

"So you didn't get a diagram of the Rule family tree mailed anonymously?"

He frowned at her, puzzled. "No. Should I have?"

"It's not important, Mr. Humphries. Now you were saying . . . ?"

"That I'm one of the heirs, and if all goes well, I'll come into quite a bit of money. That's great by me. All I want is my fair share. Just my fair share."

He paused, apparently to make sure Carol understood he was only asking what was due to him, then went on, "Suppose you'd say I've got a bit of a bee in my bonnet, but I don't trust lawyers. Never have. When I met with Ambrose Slessor about my claim on the estate, I saw straight away what a slippery piece of work he was. Thought it only wise to research the firm. In no time I decided the self-important Slessor, Slessor, Dunkling and Gold had got a lot to answer for, as I found there were any number of questionable events over the years."

"Could you be more specific?"

"No point in being specific—it's water under the bridge. The important thing is, leopards don't change their spots." He chuckled. "Sorry for the mixed metaphor, but you get what I mean. The least you could say about this particular bunch of lawyers is they've shown very poor judgment in a number of cases. Myself, I happen to believe it's closer to criminal behavior."

Giving her a lopsided, charming smile, he continued, "So you see, Inspector, I thought it my duty to advise my fellow heirs about this state of affairs. Better safe than sorry. Slessor et al are in complete control of the estate until the inheritance is settled. They could be—and I happen to believe they are—looting it."

"There are steps you can take . . ."

Humphries threw up his hands. "And I've tried, believe me! The legal fraternity in this town sticks together, no matter what. Birds of a feather, and all that. I've made complaints, but to no avail."

"Formal complaints?"

Humphries raised his shoulders. "What would be the use? The only way is safety in numbers. To speak with one voice. I've been working to get all of us on the same page."

Wondering wryly what metaphor-mixing he would accomplish next, Carol said, "You're referring to the other heirs?"

"Yes! With the exception of two. Little Ricky Webb's only twelve, so I've left him out of it, and ditto Nicholas Jordan, who's in a permanent coma. And speaking of comas, Jim Flint might as well be in one, he's so bone-headed. I tried to explain the importance of the situation, but he just stared at me like a dumb ox. Basically thick as a brick. The others were more receptive. I've talked with Fancee Porter and Chuck Inman in the States, and here in Sydney Ian Stewart and Susan Jordan." He grinned, then said with laughing ridicule, "Or should I say, *Ophelia Rule?*"

"So you were expecting a united front?"

"Something like that. Unfortunately, Fancee got herself killed."

"It must have happened around the time you saw her," said Carol pleasantly.

"I didn't see her the day she died," he said quickly. "I'd met with her the day before. In truth, I didn't know anything had happened, at least not until Chuck called me when I got back to LA. Said Fancee'd run off the road." His crooked mouth twisted a little more. "Drank like a fish when I was with her," he said with disapproval. "And it was the morning, too. Hitting the vodka like there was no tomorrow."

Kent Humphries obviously liked to give expansive answers. Carol was happy to encourage him. Garrulous behavior often led people to talk themselves into revealing more than they intended.

"Have you actually met Chuck Inman, or only spoken to him on the phone?" she asked.

He cheerfully explained how Chuck Inman had first contacted him, and later they'd met in Houston. He concluded with the accolade, "True salt of the earth type, you know."

"Mr. Inman called you first? You didn't make the initial contact?"

"I suppose I'd have to admit Chuck set everything in motion. I'd been thinking of ringing the others, but hadn't got around to it. After talking with Chuck, I realized it was up to me to do something, and he supported me one thousand percent. Chuck feels the way I do about the legal profession. Not surprising—there's more lawyers in the States than you can shake a stick at. He has this absolutely amazing collection of lawyer jokes. Want to hear a couple?"

"Not at the moment, thanks. I would like to get something clear. Whose idea was it to alert the heirs about the lawyers handling the Rule estate?"

"Mine, of course. Chuck totally supported the idea. He put me in touch with Fancee Porter. I took the ball and ran with it from there. Get your ducks in a row, I always say."

"You saw Ian Stewart recently."

"Oh, yeah, Ian Stewart." He frowned. "Conservative guy, frightened of his own shadow. Didn't really want to go up against the legal eagles, but I persuaded him to go along."

"Mr. Stewart's dead."

Kent Humphries could hardly have looked more astonished. He stared at her, slack-jawed. "What did you say?"

"Mr. Stewart committed suicide last week."

"Suicide? How?"

Carol was deliberately blunt. "Pills and a plastic bag around his neck."

Plainly taken aback by her attitude, he said, "Christ. What a way to go."

"There are a lot worse."

He swallowed. "I'm sure there are, but don't tell me about them."

"Did Mr. Stewart seem depressed when you saw him?"

"Depressed? No, not at all. He was a quiet sort, but not by any means down in the dumps. I just can't believe it . . ."

"No one who knows Mr. Stewart well seems to believe it either."

He gave her a sharp look. "Meaning what? Stewart didn't kill himself?"

"Meaning it's an open investigation."

"But it still could be suicide?" He seemed to need reassurance.

"That's very possible." Watching him closely, she added, "Jim Flint's murder yesterday may have no connection, but it does make us cautious about accepting Stewart's death at face value."

"Jesus Christ! Flint's been murdered?"

"I'm afraid so."

He got up abruptly and began to pace around the room. "Not the guy who had his throat cut? It was on the radio, but there was no name given."

"That's the one."

Humphries came to a halt, his shoulders slumping. "This is a nightmare." Then, making an obvious effort to present an unruffled demeanor, he managed an unconvincing laugh. "Hey," he said, "next you'll be telling me someone's knocking us off, one by one."

● ● ●

Friday afternoon traffic was heavy at the best of times, but an accident at the junction of Old South Head Road and Bondi Road had turned Carol's short drive back to the Police Centre into a stop-go endurance test. She took the opportunity to review the investigation the Commissioner had handed her. With Jim Flint's butchery, the tenuous idea that murder was taking place had acquired more substance.

Could it really be that all these deaths were somehow connected? Was someone behind the scenes pulling the levers, dispatching

84

those who were linked by the Rule blood? A day ago this scenario had seemed fanciful. Thurmond Rule had almost certainly died of natural causes, Martina Rule and Fancee Porter in accidents, Ian Stewart by his own hand. All these could be explained as fate. But now Jim Flint had been murdered. Suddenly being a potential heir to the Rule estate appeared to be a distinct health hazard.

And what if someone was systematically killing the heirs? Ophelia Rule had been right: the last one standing would be the person with the best motive to remove the competition. Rule had been a billionaire, and it would seem there'd be enough for everyone, but in her job Carol had seen raw greed in operation. Part of the pie was never enough for some people. They wanted it all.

If this scenario were true, the remaining heirs became the suspects. She mentally checked them off: Ricky Webb and Nicholas Jordan could both be eliminated, Ricky because of his youth, Jordan because he was comatose. Chuck Inman should have arrived in Sydney today, but when the deaths occurred he was thousands of kilometers away in Texas.

That left two: Kent Humphries and Ophelia Rule, born Susan Jordan. Ophelia had been the one to point out in her inimitable way that the heir left at the end had to be the murderer. This didn't preclude her from the role. Carol herself, if a murderer, would cheerfully play mind games just like this to establish her apparent innocence.

Kent Humphries had appeared genuinely astounded to hear of Ian Stewart's death, and shaken to the core by Jim Flint's murder. He'd been convincing, but Carol had met sociopaths who could mimic genuine emotions so well they'd fool even experienced psychiatrists. Or Humphries could simply be a gifted actor, playing a part with persuasive skill.

Premeditated murder required malice and opportunity. Ophelia Rule had the malice to commit murder—but the opportunity? Kent Humphries had the opportunity. Did he have the malice?

Of course, she thought with a grin, maybe Kent Humphries and

Ophelia Rule had combined together to rub out other heirs. Then surely, in the end, one would turn on the other. She'd put her money on Ophelia, she decided.

Her phone gave its soft chirrup. It was illegal for a driver to use a cell phone in a moving vehicle, but Carol figured the stop-and-start crawl she was in didn't really qualify as driving. "Carol Ashton."

It was Anne Newsome. Chuck Inman was on the other line wanting to know if he could see Carol in her office this afternoon. Seeing the traffic freeing up ahead of her vehicle, Carol said she'd be there in a few minutes, so to tell Inman to come right in. "And Anne, I need to speak to Les Upton."

After a pause, Upton came on. "Les, I need you to get through to Immigration . . . I know it's Friday afternoon, but give it a try. I want to know if an American citizen named Charles James Inman, also known as Chuck Inman, has entered Australia any time in the past three years. No, make that ten years."

CHAPTER EIGHT

Chuck Inman presented a surprising contrast to Carol's mental portrait. Talking to him on the phone, she'd found him a go-getter, pushy and confrontational. She'd pictured him in shiny cowboy boots, with a wide-brimmed Stetson on his head. The person who was shown into her office was a shambling, splay-footed figure wearing creased gray trousers with a mismatched darker gray suit coat. His blue shirt appeared not to have been ironed, and his loosened tie hung around his neck in a multi-colored loop.

She checked for boots. Yes, at least in that detail she'd been correct, although they scuffed and worn, and not at all the glossy pair she'd envisioned.

Inman had a thick reddish-brown hair, worn long enough to touch his collar. Ginger stubble indicated he hadn't recently shaved. He seemed entirely unfazed by his long trans-Pacific trip, as grinning broadly, he advanced with hand outstretched.

"Got off of the plane this morning, all ready to rent a car, but you Aussies drive on the wrong side of the road, you know that? So got a cab direct to the hotel, had a nap, now I'm good as new. I'm telling you, that's quite some flight. Didn't expect it to take so long." He seized her fingers in a hard grip. "And you'd be Carol. You're a good-looking lady, if you don't mind me saying so."

Knowing it was wise to establish their relative power positions immediately, Carol moved to discourage Inman's chummy informality. "Inspector Ashton, Mr. Inman."

Such reserve was not for Inman. "Chuck, Carol. Call me Chuck."

"I'd prefer to keep it formal, Mr. Inman."

A shrug. "Just being friendly."

When they were both seated, he swiveled his head around examining the room with close attention. "The same the world over," he remarked. "Could be a cop's office anywhere." He added with grating gallantry, "And your beauty shines all the brighter in contrast."

"Thank you, Mr. Inman. May I ask, have you visited Australia before?"

He spread his hands. "Everything's entirely new to me. I hear it's a wonderful, wonderful country."

As he seemed about to elaborate, Carol said hastily, "And you wanted to see me about . . . ?"

"Ambrose Slessor also speaks very highly of you." He grew solemn. "I can admit when I'm wrong. Patched a few fences today. Called Ambrose this morning and told him I spoke a trifle hastily when I said he and his partners were white-collar criminals. Asked if I could go see old Rule's mansion, being that I was going to inherit part of it. Looks quite a building in photos, and on the waterfront, too. You've got a world class harbor here, you know."

Carol groaned to herself. She'd thought Humphries garrulous, but there was no contest. This guy could talk the legs off an iron pot.

"What did Mr. Slessor say?" she asked, hoping to cut the story short.

"Ambrose said no. Told me why. The court hasn't had its say yet. I get his drift, but I just might mosey down there and have a look."

"Mr. Inman—"

"Wanting me to get to the point? Spoke to Kent Humphries this afternoon. Said you'd just left his apartment. I was shocked when he told me Ian Stewart is no longer with us. Killed himself."

"It appears to be the case."

"And then Kent said Jimmy Flint had been murdered by person or persons unknown." He shook his head so hard his hair swirled around his head. "Warned you, didn't I? Said something was screwy."

"Perhaps you'll explain."

Inman beamed at her. "Classy lady, playing your cards close to your chest. Letting me do the talking."

Carol waited. Inman nodded to himself. "Don't underestimate this one, Chuck. She'll hang you out to dry."

"Colorful," said Carol, "but not accurate. Now, you were saying something struck you as odd?"

"It's a pattern. Amazed you can't see it." He held up three thick fingers. "A three-part plan: one, get Rule's daughter. Two, wait for the genuine claimants to get in line. Three, start picking them off. Fancee, Stewart, Flint. Who knows who's next?"

"Wouldn't there be a fourth part to the scheme? The payoff for the murderer?"

"Money, money, money," he half-sang. Carol imagined Inman breaking into Abba's hit song, if given any encouragement at all.

"Mr. Inman, the scenario you've described suggests the murderer—if, indeed there is a murderer—should be found among the remaining heirs. That would make you a suspect."

89

Inman threw back his head and laughed heartily. Wiping his eyes, he declared, "I only entered your fair country this morning, Inspector. When Jimmy Flint died, I guess I was flying over the wide blue sea."

"One doesn't have to do one's own killing," Carol observed.

He clicked his tongue at her comment. "Never use a third party, I say. When the chips are down, they'll always rat you out. Do it yourself, or don't do it at all."

"For the sake of argument, let's say your theory's correct, Mr. Inman. Do you have an idea of who might be the guilty party?"

"You know, I could listen to you Aussies talk for hours. Great accent."

"So you have no one in mind?"

"Eric Rule." He leaned back with a satisfied grunt.

Not altogether surprised, as Vida Drake had already raised the implausible suggestion that Eric Rule was stalking the heirs, Carol said, "Thurmond Rule's son? He disappeared long ago, and has been declared officially dead."

"Officially dead is not necessarily dead, dead. In fact, he's very much in the land of the living."

Dubious, Carol said, "You have evidence that Eric Rule is still alive?"

Pleased with himself, Inman declared, "I have."

"Have you informed Mr. Slessor? As trustee for the Rule estate, he must immediately be advised if a direct relative has been found."

"Not found, exactly." He leaned forward confidentially. "Your police department here—do you use psychics? I'm sure you do but don't admit it."

A wave of irritation washed over Carol. She had a report for the Commissioner to finish, with a copy to Superintendent Edgar. Then there was Aunt Sarah, who was luring her home with the promise of a good, old-fashioned roast beef dinner. And here was this American, holding her up, chattering on about psychics.

Her voice cool, she said, "It's not Police Service policy to use psychics."

90

Inman slapped the palm of his hand on her desk top. "You can level with me. I know how it is. Nothing official, but behind the scenes . . ." He winked knowingly.

In her job Carol had had occasional experience with psychics, and had become wary of their involvement in cases. Often these people were called in as a last resort by frantic parents distraught because of a missing child. There'd been a couple of times when Carol had been surprised by information provided through these non-conventional means, but generally she found the whole thing a depressing example of desperate hopes overwhelming pragmatic good sense.

"Concerning Eric Rule, you've spoken with a psychic?" she said, hoping her cynicism wasn't too obvious. Perhaps he sincerely believed paranormal powers.

"Employed her myself. Thought it worth the money. Excellent woman. Great track record. Been on television in the States. Perhaps you've heard of her? Katarina Thane?"

"I don't recall the name."

"Katarina knew immediately Eric Rule wasn't dead."

I'm not having this conversation, Carol thought. "I'd need hard evidence, Mr. Inman."

"Ah, a skeptic? Me too. Total skeptic. But there's something about Katarina that convinces. You'd feel the same way if you met her. Lovely young woman. And as I said, a wonderful track record. Found murdered bodies when nobody else could. Brought closure to countless families."

"Where is Eric Rule?" said Carol. "In America?"

"No, no. He never left Australia. Katarina says he changed his identity, and drifted around the country for years." Noticing Carol's expression of disbelief, he went on, "You know, time and space make no difference to a true psychic. It was totally incredible the way she absorbed Eric's thoughts and feelings."

Carol wanted this conversation over fast, but heard herself saying, "Why did Eric disappear? And when his father died, why not come out of hiding and claim the money? Why go around killing would-be heirs, when he, as Thurmond Rule's son, has absolute right to the entire estate?"

"You'll have to ask Eric when you arrest him," said Inman. "I hope I have your word you'll put out an APB for him immediately."

Carol could imagine what would happen to her career if she took such a lunatic step. "Without concrete evidence that Eric Rule is even alive, I can't possibly do that."

Abruptly, Inman got to his feet. "Well, we don't see eye to eye on that!" He moved toward the door. "I've been taking up too much of your valuable time already."

Carol stood too, buoyed with relief the man was finally leaving. "I'll see you out."

At the top of the stairs Chuck Inman turned to her. "I won't be asking for police protection," he said, "even though I'm convinced I'm a target. I'm making my own arrangements. Ambrose Slessor put me on to Fred Verrell. Believe you know him."

An image of Fred Verrell, complete with his small, black poodle, Nero, habitually carried under one arm, rose in Carol's mind. Verrell and his poodle guarding Chuck Inman? The idea was risible.

"Fred Verrell's your bodyguard?"

"Not Fred, exactly, although he'll be there for my high-profile appearances. A couple of other guys, Ledmark and Gallagher, will be with me most of the time."

"David Ledmark?"

He nodded. "That's the man."

Walking back to her office, Carol thought of Fred Verrell with distaste. She'd smiled to herself at the concept of Fred Verrell as a bodyguard, but in person he was not amusing. Infuriating would be a better word, in Carol's opinion.

A cocky little man, Verrell had mastered the art of coercion of underlings, combined with stomach-turning toadying where his clients were concerned. His lack of height clearly galled him. He had lifts in his shoes, and he habitually stood bolt upright, chest out, chin high, to gain that extra centimeter. She'd noticed how he avoided standing next to her, or indeed, anyone much taller than he was, particularly if the person happened to be female.

She was deep in thought when, to get her attention, Les Upton plucked at Carol as she made her way past his desk. Managing with an effort not to deliver a sharp slap to his hand, Carol said, "What is it, Les?"

"Liam Doherty, the witness to the accident that killed the Rule woman—he's disappeared. Lived in the same boarding house for six years, then one day he's gone, leaving all his things behind."

"Missing persons been notified?"

"Eventually. His landlady finally went to the local cops and wants to know what she's to do with Doherty's stuff. They do a quick check of unidentified bodies, admissions to hospitals. Nothing. The guy walked out one day and vanished."

Carol felt a tingle of disquiet, as she herself had investigated Martina Rule's death. Had she been too hasty to take the apparent accident at face value? "What about the driver of the truck, Sid Hawkins?"

"Hawkins is out of the country. Never traveled before because his handyman business didn't make all that much. Then suddenly he lets it be known he's come into some hard cash. In short order he's wound up his business, and left for Bali. Last report has him living it up big time."

Les Upton had the expression of one who is holding one more winning card. Carol, resigned to bad news, said, "What else?"

"Hawkins and Doherty were supposed to be complete strangers. Handy, because it made Doherty much more convincing as a witness. Fact is, though, they weren't. Both belong to the Eastern Suburbs Rugby League Club. When I discovered Hawkins was a member, I checked for Doherty's name. Surprise! They joined at the same time, almost a year ago."

The club supported the Roosters, the professional rugby league football team representing the eastern suburbs of Sydney. Like similar football clubs, it provided a social center for the membership, offering a wide range of amenities, including weight and exercise gyms, bars, restaurants, and for fund-raising, legal gambling on poker machines. That both men belonged to the club was interesting, but the fact they'd joined at the same time was a red flag.

"Okay, Les, locate exactly where Hawkins is in Bali. I'll have him interrogated there, and possibly arrange to have him extradited."

Upton looked mildly surprised. "On what charge?"

"Let's try murder."

The unsettling feeling events were starting to escalate out of her control sharpened Carol's voice. "I want you to work with Anne on this. We need to know if anyone associated with Thurmond Rule or his daughter had any connection to Hawkins or Doherty. And if it's a conspiracy to murder, then these two guys were well paid for their work, so look for a money trail."

This particular club, Carol recalled, was at Bondi Junction, in the same suburb in which Kent Humphries lived. "And Les, check if any of the Rule heirs have anything to do with that same club. Anne will give you the names."

Upton's expression brightened. "This is going to be fun."

This type of dogged research, where blind alleys led to blind alleys, and only a few leads had useful payoffs, had never been Carol's idea of an enjoyable activity. "As long as you're happy in your work, Les," she said. "What's happening about Chuck Inman?"

"Immigration hasn't got back to me yet. I'd reckon I won't hear until Monday at the earliest."

"If you don't get action first thing on Monday morning, lean on Immigration hard. Tell them the Commissioner needs it urgently. And the moment you have the information, let me have it."

Anne was in the cramped little kitchen dunking a teabag in hot water. "Want a cup of tea?" she asked. "Guaranteed to be an improvement on our coffee."

"No tea, thanks. Les has turned up some information on Martina Rule's death." She briefly summarized Upton's findings and the need to establish any links between the two men and anyone associated with the Rules.

"You're thinking murder?" said Anne.

"It looks that way."

"Martina's father a victim too?"

Carol grimaced. "That one goes to the too-hard basket. There's no doubt Rule had advanced pancreatic cancer. When he died he was on heavy doses of morphine. Perhaps somebody did give him a fatal injection, but who's to say it's murder or just a kindly hastening of inevitable death? The body's been cremated, so unless someone is suddenly wracked with guilt, and confesses, his death remains on the books as a natural one."

Anne sipped her tea thoughtfully. "Who benefits from Martina Rule's death?" Answering her own question, she said, "Not Juanita Paz, who lost her chance at three hundred thou when the will was changed. But the distant Rule relatives are vastly better off, since Martina stood in the way of their considerable inheritance."

"The amount of money isn't always the indicator," said Carol, thinking of cases where murder had been committed for paltry amounts by most people's standards.

"I saw Chuck Inman come in," said Anne. "He made quite an impression on me."

"He complimented you on your looks?"

Anne grinned. "I can tell you I haven't been called a little lady for quite some time."

"Mr. Inman believes he's in danger, so he's got himself a body-guard, who just happens to be your new friend, David Ledmark. You might say I'm officially encouraging you to contact him. See what you can find out."

"Any particular angle?"

Carol lifted a shoulder. "I'm not sure what I'm looking for. Just use your instincts." Smiling, she tapped the constable lightly on the shoulder. "Not necessarily *all* your instincts, Anne, though Mr. Ledmark does have a certain sex appeal . . ."

Leaving Anne laughing, Carol located Miles Li at his desk, and gave him the task of finding the American psychic Inman had mentioned, Katarina Thane. "She's sure to have a website, Miles. See if you can track her down." Then she went back to her desk to finish the report for the Commissioner. She'd been updating the file as information came to hand. As she typed Ophelia Rule's name, her hands stilled on the keyboard. After a moment's thought, she checked a number and made a call.

"This is Inspector Carol Ashton, Ms. Rule."

Before she could say anything more, Ophelia snapped, "Chuck called me. Says he saw you and you weren't much bloody help."

"Mr. Inman told you about Jim Flint?"

"He sure did. What are you going to do, eh? Stewart's gone. Flint's gone. You're planning to wait until we're all bloody dead before you get off your fat behind and do something?"

"I'm afraid it's all conjecture at the moment. If there's any hard evidence, of course I'll act immediately. Up until then, I can't legally do anything."

"So exactly why are you calling?"

"To ask about the security at the long-term care facility where your brother is a patient."

"Nick? He doesn't know whether it's day or night."

"As long as he's alive, your brother can still inherit. It will go into his estate, and no doubt be administered by you, but he's still an heir."

"What are you saying?" demanded Ophelia. "Someone might go in and turn the machines off?"

"Just as a precaution, I'm suggesting you might take steps to alert the facility there may be a need for heightened security."

"Nice you so keen to protect a virtual vegetable, but what about me?" Ophelia bellowed down the phone. "I don't hear you warning me to look out for myself."

"It would be wise if you, Mr. Humphries and Mr. Inman are all very careful about where you go and who you see."

She snorted derisively. "Chuck's convinced Eric Rule's stalking us."

"Mr. Inman's relying on information obtained from a psychic," said Carol in a non-committal tone.

Ophelia blew a raspberry. "Psychic!" she said with scorn. "Don't hold with all that woo woo stuff. Fucking stupid, if you ask me."

● ● ●

As Carol was leaving, particularly fatigued after having fielded with gritted-teeth charm a number of media inquiries about her investigations regarding the Rule family, Les Upton stopped her. "Something you'll really want to know. Sid Hawkins was knifed to death in a brawl outside a Bali nightclub two months ago. No arrests, and not likely to be any. It was a general free-for-all, and when the cops turned up, everyone ran." He gave a tight smile. "Except, of course, the ones who couldn't, like Hawkins."

It was bliss to be alone in her car. Carol knew she'd enjoy the drive home, even though roads were congested with Friday evening traffic. Soon she'd relish swooping down the long hill that gave breathtaking views of Middle Harbour and the Spit, and then the climb up the other side, the escape into peaceful streets. She'd draw up at her home, perched high above the water, surrounded by eucalyptus gum trees. She'd turn off the engine, and a quieter world would rush in to fill the space—the murmur of wind in the leaves, the sleepy sounds from birds settling in for the night.

Stuck in a line of slow cars, and still four kilometers from home, she used the time to run over the latest developments in the investigation. The convenient death of Hawkins and the disappearance of Doherty made it even more likely Martina Rule had been deliberately killed. If it hadn't been an accident, there were a number of new possibilities. Perhaps she'd been eliminated for some reason entirely separate from the fortune she was set to inherit. A jealous lover? Unpaid bills for a drug habit? Somebody vicious she'd crossed in her short but tempestuous life?

Financial advantage or personal hatred were the two compelling motives for murder. There was always a key question to ask: who benefits? There were plenty of people who had reason to dislike Martina, but no one stood out as a candidate for committing premeditated homicide. This killing had been meticulously planned. It was not violence unleashed in the spur of the moment. Someone had persuaded Hawkins and Doherty to be the key players in a scheme to disguise Martina Rule's death as a pedestrian accident, a scheme so well thought out and executed, it had nearly succeeded.

Chuck Inman's comment, "Do it yourself, or don't do it at all," was advice many convicted murderers should have heeded. When you contracted out a killing, there were two ever-present risks. First, the person you hired might slip up, be arrested, and then implicate you. Second, you were leaving yourself open to the very real threat of blackmail. Murder was almost always better accomplished as a do-it-yourself activity.

As Carol went back over the day, she suddenly realized how much, despite its frustrations and demands, she loved her job. It was the threat of losing it, she thought, that had brought this home to her. She remembered Sybil once saying, with a thread of bitterness, "Carol, you are your job: your job is you." At the time Carol had dismissed this as a flippant dig at the long hours she was putting in at work, but now she saw the comment in a different light. It was true, she had to admit. In many ways her job defined whom she was.

At last freed from the knotted traffic, Carol enjoyed the last few minutes of her drive through leafy suburban streets. She parked in her street-level carport, waved to her neighbor, calling out that she'd take Olga, the neighbor's German shepherd, for the usual bushland run early the next day. Pressure of work had meant Carol had not run for several mornings, and she was missing the surge of energy the exercise always gave her.

She unloaded her briefcase from the boot of the car, then paused at her gate. Standing here, looking down at her house and garden, gently lit by fading light, she felt a rush of ownership. How could she ever leave?

It was delightful to open the front door and have the mouth-watering smell of Aunt Sarah's cooking fill her nose. Roast beef with all the trimmings would always be one of her favorite meals.

Her aunt welcomed her with a hug. Carol stood back and looked her up and down. Accustomed to seeing her aunt in her signature apparel, a rainbow collection of colored overalls, it was a surprise to find her in more somber wear. "You're wearing black?"

"Black's slimming, darling, and I do want to look my best for my portrait showing. I had it made in Bangkok. Wonderful tailor ran it up in a couple of hours." She twirled around. "What do you think? Too severe?"

"You look adorable." Drawn by the smell of dinner, Carol set off in the direction of the kitchen.

"Perhaps I could set it off with red shoes. Or maybe a purple scarf."

"You're going to look terrific, whatever you do."

Reaching the kitchen, Carol was waylaid by the black and white Sinker, who'd obviously been waiting for her to arrive. He gave her a blank feline stare, punctuated by one imperious meow, somehow managing to convey clearly he was starving, neglected, and frankly, just wasn't going to take it any more.

"He's manipulating you, dear," said Aunt Sarah as Carol hastened to get his food. "Cats do that so well. I didn't want to spoil his fun, so I didn't try to feed him."

With Sinker satisfied, Carol got herself a Scotch and her aunt a dry sherry. "It's so great having you here," she said when Aunt Sarah came back from changing into a lime green smock.

"That's your stomach talking," was the dry reply. "And you can repay me for all this tender loving care by promising you'll come to the cocktail party for my portrait showing next Friday. Parking's a bit hard at Sybil's place, but I'm sure everyone will manage. It's going to be a big success. My Eco-Crones are renting a bus and driving down together from the Blue Mountains, Yancey's got some artist types coming, and Sybil's got teacher friends lined up. Since you're my only niece, I'm expecting you to be there too. I've already asked Pat and Mark Bourke, and that nice Anne Newsome will try and make it. Put it in your diary as a must-do engagement. Seven-thirty next Friday."

"I'll try."

"Not good enough, Carol. I don't want you using some dead body as an excuse, either."

"I'm in the homicide squad. Dead bodies are my business."

Aunt Sarah gave her a long, serious look. "What will your business be if you move to the States?"

"I haven't even had time to think about the possibility."

Aunt Sarah's expression indicated she didn't consider that an adequate answer, but she didn't comment, instead directing Carol to carve the meat while she made gravy the old-fashioned way in the pan with juice from the meat combined with flour and water.

Stirring vigorously, she said over her shoulder, "Sybil and Yancey are having some difficulties with their relationship. It's even possible they may break up."

The timing of this remark put Carol on full alert. "Nothing to do with me."

"I never said it was, dear. Merely thought you might be interested."

"Not particularly."

"Sybil hasn't said anything to you?"

Carol could answer this with complete truthfulness. "Not one word."

Her aunt gave her a mocking smile. "Not one word? And you and Sybil becoming such good friends again . . ."

When Carol didn't deign to reply, she went on, "While Sybil was here this afternoon, we got talking about Yancey and my portrait. One thing led to another, and she told me about the difficulties she and Yancey were having."

"Sybil was here?"

"Don't sound so surprised. I asked her to call in after school to run through the arrangements for Friday. I'm in charge of the food. Fortunately I've got several Eco-Crones contributing. Sybil's looking after the wine etcetera." She cocked her head. "You don't mind Sybil coming here, do you?"

"Of course not."

"Aren't you going to ask me any questions?"

"I wasn't planning to."

"You're being difficult, darling, but I should have expected you would be where Sybil's concerned."

The restful evening she'd envisaged was rapidly disappearing. "You never give up, Aunt Sarah, do you?" she said with an edge in her voice.

"I know you, Carol—"

"Then you know I don't want to discuss Sybil, or Yancey, or the cocktail party. It's your portrait, I'm proud of you, and I'd like to be there for you. We don't need to say another word on the topic. Okay?"

"Hmmm," murmured her aunt. Carol hoped it meant the subject was closed, but she wasn't at all sanguine this was the case.

After a pause, Aunt Sarah said, "I spoke with Leota today. She'll be calling this evening to confirm, but hopes to make it to Sydney before lunch tomorrow."

With a mischievous smile, she added, "Knowing you two would rather be alone, I've arranged with Hazel Foster to stay at her place for the weekend. She's picking me up in the morning. You remember Hazel, don't you, Carol? Before she moved down here from the mountains, she held our Crone record for arrests."

"This is something to be proud of?"

Aunt Sarah smiled in reminiscence. "I can tell you the Eco-Crones miss Hazel's contribution to our cause. She specialized in flinging herself on the ground at our demos, and playing dead. Carrying a bit of weight, Hazel is, and it usually took at least two cops to carry her away. Had her photograph featured in the paper several times."

After dinner, when the phone rang, Aunt Sarah said, "That'll be Leota. Did I mention I asked her to my portrait showing? No? I must have forgotten."

Carol made a face at her as she picked up the receiver. The timing of this information was suspicious, as in her experience, her aunt rarely forgot anything.

"Carol, honey," said Leota. "I can't wait to see you. I'm driving up from Canberra, and should make it to your place mid-morning. If you're working, don't worry. I'll amuse myself."

"I'm on a case, but I'll make time." Carol paused, then said, "Darling . . ."

"Yes?"

"Oh, I don't know. Just darling."

Leota gave her soft laugh. "See you tomorrow."

She replaced the receiver and turned to her aunt. "Why did you ask Leota to the cocktail party?"

"I was sure she'd be interested in seeing my portrait. And I was right. She accepted the invitation without a moment's thought."

"That airy tone doesn't fool me, Aunt Sarah. You're up to something."

"I'm wondering why you feel so defensive, darling."

Carol knew her aunt liked Leota very much, but she still regarded Sybil as a member of the family. She'd made no secret of her distress when Carol and Sybil had broken up. Carol suspected she nursed hopes of them getting together again.

"This isn't your idea of some kind of bizarre comparison test between Leota and Sybil, is it?"

"Of course not. I thought it was high time they met, as they both have a common interest"—an ingenuous smile—"namely you, Carol."

Before she could respond, the phone rang again. When Carol answered it, she repressed an impatient sigh. "How did you get this number, Vida?"

"I'm a journalist, for God's sake. We have our methods."

"Is this a matter of urgency? If not, I suggest we talk on Monday. I'm sure you understand I prefer not to be interrupted at home."

Carol's cold, unwelcoming voice failed to deter the journalist. "I've just done an interview with Chuck Inman. *Very* interesting. I'm giving you the opportunity to comment."

Knowing that Vida Drake was quite capable of recording their conversation, and then quoting responses out of context, Carol chose her words with care. "As I've neither heard nor seen the interview, I'm not in a position to comment."

"Sharp answer," said Vida. "At least give me your response on Chuck Inman's hypothesis Eric Rule is still alive, and is stalking the heirs to his father's fortune."

"We evaluate all hypotheses in the light of credible evidence to support them."

Vida snickered. "Does using a psychic's insights count as credible evidence?"

"No comment."

"Don't be frightened I'll misquote you, Carol. You can tell me exactly what you think of Chuck's little theory."

"Thank you, Vida," said Carol dryly, "that's reassuring."

"The heirs keep popping off, don't they? Quite shocking, Jim Flint's very violent death. I hear his throat was slit from ear to ear. Assuming you're not looking for Eric Rule, do you have other suspects?"

"The investigation's proceeding. No other comment."

In a wounded tone, Vida Drake said, "May I remind you when we had coffee on Wednesday, you pledged full cooperation. So where is it?"

"I promised no such thing. What I did say was you'd be one of the first to be advised of developments. I've nothing to give you yet."

"So your investigation's stalled? What does the Commissioner think of that? Do you think he'd make a statement?"

"I suggest you contact his publicity office."

"Are you planning to make a statement to the media about the Rule case soon? Or will Superintendent Edgar steal your thunder again?"

"I've no doubt there'll be a statement when we have something definitive to say."

"You're stonewalling," said Vida with asperity. "Don't count on me giving up, Carol. You'll find yourself answering my questions sooner or later. Might as well be sooner, don't you think?"

"You should meet my Aunt Sarah," said Carol. "You've got a lot in common."

CHAPTER NINE

Lying in bed, lazily intertwined, the late afternoon sun slanting through the windows and pooling on the floor, was Carol's idea of perfect peace.

Leota said, "What are you thinking?"

Carol ran her hand down the satiny skin of Leota's flank. "How nicely we contrast."

Carol was lightly tanned, but she looked very pale beside Leota's darker hue.

In unspoken accord, they hadn't discussed the future, but now Leota said, "I'd find it very hard to live without you."

"I was thinking the same."

"Honey, I know it's a daunting thing to ask of you, to leave your country and come with me." She stopped Carol's response with a finger across her lips. "Don't say anything. Just listen. Your happiness is everything to me. If I didn't think it would work out, I'd never suggest you make the move."

"There are so many things to consider."

Leota slid her hand between Carol's legs. "There's this, for instance." She turned slightly, to take a nipple into the warmth of her mouth. Languidly, she began to tease it with her tongue.

Carol's tranquil body began slowly to fill with delightful tension. She slipped her fingers inside Leota, plunging indolently into the smooth wetness, stroking, implacable, until Leota gasped.

They made unhurried love, measured and deliberate, bringing each other to the brink, but never tipping over. Carol felt herself floating in a relentless, burning sea of sensation. On and on it went, never cresting, until abruptly, it was unbearable.

"Now!"

Everything faded into a screaming silence. She rose, quivering, vibrating. Exploded into shards of light.

Smiling against Leota's lips, she whispered, "You play me like a violin, you know."

Leota laughed. "Your *glissando* is good, but I particularly admire your *crescendo*," she said.

• • •

"Am I interrupting anything?" asked Maureen Oatland.

Carol stroked Leota's cheek. "Not a thing."

Through the line she could hear muffled voices in the background and the trill of a phone. With a stab of guilt she realized Maureen was in the office, while she was sprawled, satiated, with her lover.

Swinging her legs over the side of the bed, Carol reached for a robe. "What've you got, Maureen?"

"I'll give you the short version. Last night at the pub, I chatted up a motley bunch of guys. Most of them knew Flint, probably because of his tendency to have one beer too many and turn nasty. No one admitted to seeing him drinking with anyone in particular. No one saw him leave. The news of his unfortunate end had spread like wildfire, and I got quite a few questions about how exactly he'd died, but there was a conspicuous lack of grief at his passing."

"What about the door-to-door?" Carol asked.

"Nothing of substance, except for one old bloke whose house overlooks the pub's parking lot. I went and saw him myself. On Thursday night about ten he thought he might have seen a guy who could have been Flint with another person. They were near a truck parked at the back of the lot. Not sure if this other person was male or female. He didn't remember the vehicle's color. His eyesight's not so good and he'd been hitting the booze himself, so I'd reckon he's not the most reliable witness."

"When you think how many people were in that pub," said Carol, "it's hard to believe no one saw anything."

"I've left a supply of my business cards with the owner, and asked him to hand them out to any regular patrons who didn't make it last night. I told him, concentrate on the really good-looking ones." Maureen gave a hoot of laughter. "He didn't crack a smile, just gave me an odd look, so I had to explain I was joking."

"And were you?" Carol inquired.

"Of course. I can do better. Or so I tell myself."

Maureen's jovial tone became more serious as she continued, "Attended Jim Flint's post mortem this morning. The usual blood and guts with Jeff Duke playing opera while he worked. Not sure why, but I found the whole thing more gruesome than usual. There's something about a cut throat . . . Anyway, time of death was somewhere between ten on Thursday night and two on Friday morning. The incision was made from left to right."

"Too awkward a maneuver from the passenger seat," said Carol, "so the murderer either opened the driver's door, or leaned in through the window. That would make him right-handed."

"Did a good job," said Maureen. "No hope of survival even if medical care had been there on the spot. Flint bled out in two or three minutes. No defensive wounds on his hands. And the reason he sat there and let it happen? Besides the fact he'd been drinking, someone had jabbed him with a hypodermic on the left side of his neck. No lab tests available yet, but Jeff's betting whatever it was knocked Flint out completely. He would never have known his throat was being slashed."

"The weapon?"

"A thin knife or scalpel, very sharp. And Liz Carey reports no fingerprints, not even the victim's, in the truck. Someone had wiped the cabin clean. And no prints on the whiskey bottle on the floor. Liz is setting up DNA tests on the bottle, just in case someone shared it with him and left traces of saliva, but it's a long shot."

"Anything else of use at the crime scene?"

"Nothing useful inside the truck, including the glove box, which only had a flashlight and a street directory. Outside the vehicle there were no footprints, no tire marks."

"Someone planned this well," Carol said.

"I'll say, though they ran a risk I wouldn't take. As Flint was found behind the wheel, the best guess is he drove his own truck to where it was found. They're bloody lucky he didn't run into something, or get picked up for drunk driving on the way."

"Mr. Flint's record shows he has a lot of practice at driving while drunk," said Carol sardonically.

"So here's my take on the murder," said Maureen. "Flint's encouraged to drive to the privacy of the dead-end street by the promise of something—drugs, sex, whatever. If it's sex it probably means there's a woman with him, although we both know how many supposed heteros swing both ways."

"Any evidence of sexual activity?"

A cackle from Maureen. "Did he have one for the road before he carked it? Jeff says no. He's just sitting there, having a companionable slug or two of whiskey, and everything's fine. Suddenly, bam! A quick jab of a needle into his neck, and he's totally out of it. The murderer takes time to wipe down any surfaces where fingerprints could be, hops out of the truck, walks around to the other side, leans in, cuts Flint's throat, then gets out of there."

"Whoever was with Flint in the truck needed transport to get away. Why not have an accomplice follow, and then park out of sight? It could be the accomplice who waits until the signal comes that Flint's unconscious. He then opens the driver's door and kills him."

"An accomplice isn't necessary," said Maureen. "He could have left a car parked nearby. Or—and this is my favorite theory—the perp puts a bicycle in the back of the truck, and pedals off into the night after doing the deed."

• • •

On Sunday morning Carol reluctantly left Leota and went into the Centre to meet Mark Bourke. He arrived with a box of assorted doughnuts and a two paper cups of excellent coffee. Under his arm was a neatly folded newspaper.

"Seen this?" he asked, handing it to her with a quizzical grin. "Your friend Vida Drake has made the front page."

A FAMILY CURSED? the headline inquired. Underneath, in a slightly smaller typeface was: *A FORTUNE WAITS WHILE HEIRS SQUABBLE—AND DIE.*

"Squabble?" said Carol. "What's that about?"

"Vida Drake snagged an interview with Ophelia Rule. She wasn't quoted directly—no doubt because every utterance veers far too close to libel—but the general gist was clear. Apparently, according to Ophelia, everybody's trying to screw her out of her fair share, including the solicitors. Blood-sucking leeches and vampires, she calls them. Actually Vida has edited Ophelia's words rather cunningly, so the statement becomes a blanket denunciation of crooked lawyers, but reading between the lines, it's Slessor, Slessor, Dunkling and Gold all the way. On top of that, she's spitting chips because she claims some unnamed heir has unkindly suggested

109

Ophelia is deliberately prolonging her brother's suffering so she can get her hands on his portion of the inheritance."

"With a mouth like hers, it's a wonder to me the woman's never been sued."

Bourke looked smug. "I got Miles to check, and I'm delighted to say she has been, several times. All settled out of court, and not to her advantage. Plus she had such a brouhaha with the insurance company covering worker's compensation for her brother after his accident, she held up the resolution of the claim for months and months, and while waiting, had to fork out a small fortune for his care out of her own pocket."

"The accident was above board?" No one had suggested otherwise, but Carol was becoming leery of anything even remotely connected to the Rule family.

"Miles checked that too, and it was. Jordan simply got careless on scaffolding, slipped and fell. At least ten of his workmates witnessed it. The curse of the Rules wasn't in operation in this case."

Fearing his reply, Carol said, "Do I get a mention anywhere in the article, Mark?"

"You certainly do." Bourke took the paper from her, scanned for a moment, then read aloud, "High-profile Detective Inspector Carol Ashton heads a task force desperately searching for answers, but baffled at every turn. This reporter recalls at Martina Rule's inquest, Ashton was adamant the heiress's death was an unfortunate accident. In the light of recent events, perhaps she might reconsider this rush to judgment."

"Oh, great," said Carol. "I can't wait until Edgar gets in tomorrow."

She didn't have to wait that long. Her mobile phone rang in her briefcase. When she fished it out, Superintendent Edgar's voice boomed in her ear. "Have you read this absolute tripe in the Sunday paper today? Where does this Drake woman get off? Baffled at every turn! Rush to judgment, indeed! This type of publicity reflects badly, very badly on the Police Service, Carol. I want you to get cracking, put to rest these doubts the press is raising."

Carol made appropriate noises, listened to another lecture about the damage such reporting could do to the public's confidence in law enforcement, and when Superintendent Edgar finally ran out of steam, was able to ring off.

"The super at his best," she said dryly when Bourke made a sympathetic face at her. "Let's get to work before the general public loses even more faith in us."

She brought Bourke up to date on all that had happened while he'd been in South Australia. He chortled at Chuck Inman's theory about Eric Rule, as revealed by psychic Katarina Thane. Then she asked him what he'd discovered about Ricky Webb's family and the dreadful accident that had left Ricky an orphan.

Between mouthfuls of chocolate doughnut, Bourke said, "This is fascinating, Carol. I've checked with my favorite genealogist, and she says Ricky's mother, Rosalie Webb, would have had a somewhat better case as a claimant than any of the others, once Martina Rule was out of the way."

"So if Rosalie Webb had still been alive after Martina was killed and Thurmond Rule died, the courts would rule Rosalie was the principal heir?"

"Quite possibly." Bourke peered into the doughnut box and selected another. "And that means most, if not all of the more distant relatives—that is, the present applicants—would have weaker claims. There was a possibility the bulk of the estate would go to Rosalie. To be efficient, three of the four Webbs had to be killed because they were in line to inherit. The father obviously was no blood relation, so his death was collateral damage, but Rosalie and her two children, Ricky and a baby, Penny, had to go."

"But Ricky Webb survived."

Bourke grimaced. "Saved by a stomach ache. Apparently he was most upset to be left behind when the rest of the family went off for a nice day on the water. Unfortunately, the galley of the boat was full of butane gas from the pressurized canister feeding the stove. When someone when down to prepare lunch, boom! Huge explosion. Rosalie Webb, Peter Webb and Penny Webb died instantly. The vessel burnt to the waterline."

Carol pushed away the image of a baby's little body floating in the debris of the explosion. "Was there any suggestion at the time that it wasn't an accident?"

"The butane gas container had been refilled by Peter Webb the day before and put back in the boat. The coroner ruled it was an accidental leakage, probably caused by a connection not being sufficiently tightened. I don't like our chances of finding evidence it was a deliberate set up to murder the family, although several witnesses did emphasize how Peter Webb had always been very particular about safety."

Carol sighed. "Now I'm worried about Ricky Webb's safety."

Bourke nodded. "Me too. That's why I had a talk to the Reverend Ackland and his wife, who have taken Ricky into their family. I stressed it was totally unofficial, but they needed to know I had some concerns about Ricky's safety. They were very cooperative, and agreed to move him to an undisclosed location until I gave them the all clear."

Carol always tried to ration herself to one doughnut, but found herself reaching for a second. Seeing her hesitate, Bourke said, "Oh, go on, give in to temptation. You're stressed. You need the sugar."

"Get thee behind me, Satan," said Carol, grinning at him. She got up, grabbed a marking pen, and went to the whiteboard. "Let's put everything in chronological order. First, Thurmond Rule. If you're plotting to eliminate rival heirs, there's no point unless you expect the Rule billions to become available for inheritance.

"According to Dr. McMinn, Rule learns he has cancer eighteen months before he dies. The fact he's mortally ill is kept quiet. He fights the disease, and doesn't begin to show signs of succumbing until a few months before the end."

"So who knew he was dying? And when did they know?" Bourke said.

"Those are the key questions, Mark. There's no motive to kill the Webb family unless the murderer knows the Rule fortune is up for grabs. Five months before Thurmond Rule dies, most of the Webb family is wiped out, so someone was aware it was fatal cancer before that date."

"So Martina's left," said Bourke, "and she has to be removed before her father dies."

"Whoever it is certainly cut it close. She's killed in an apparent accident only a couple of weeks before his death."

She drew an arrow off to the side and printed Hawkins and Doherty's names. "The witness to the accident, Liam Doherty, disappears. Whereabouts unknown. I wouldn't be surprised to find he's buried in some lonely grave. Sid Hawkins, the driver of the vehicle, comes into money and zips off to Bali to live the good life, where some months later he's knifed in a brawl outside a nightclub."

Warming to the task, Bourke said, "Meanwhile, in Texas, Fancee Porter runs into a tree and dies. Shortly thereafter, Ian Stewart apparently kills himself. Last Thursday Jim Flint has his throat cut by villains unknown."

Carol printed the names of the heirs still living: Kent Humphries, Chuck Inman, Nicholas Jordan, Sue Jordan a.k.a. Ophelia Rule, Ricky Webb.

"Two can be ruled out as suspects," said Bourke. "Nicholas Blake because he's incapable, and Ricky Webb because he's a kid. And by the way, Carol, in light of your comments about Ricky's new family wanting him to inherit a lot of money, I did look narrowly at the Reverend Ackland and his wife. Couldn't find a nefarious bone in either body. Of course, I'm easily fooled, as you know."

"I've noticed." She drew lines through Jordan and Ricky Webb's names. "So we have three left. Who's your best bet?"

"If Fancee Porter's death was murder, then only Inman or Humphries were in the States at the time. Of course, that doesn't rule out paying someone else to make the hit, so Ophelia could have accomplished it long distance. Only you have had the pleasure of meeting Chuck and Kent. I do, however, know Ophelia. To know her is not to love her. Call me biased, but she's my choice du jour."

113

"But is she smart enough? Plus, all of this has taken a great deal of preparation and planning. One person couldn't accomplish it all. Can you really visualize anyone working cooperatively long-term with Ophelia Rule?"

"You haven't taken something vital into account," Bourke admonished her. "The promise of enough money can buy anything, even, pity help us all, collaboration with the fearsome Ophelia."

CHAPTER TEN

Monday morning Carol tore herself away from Leota's arms and left for the office even earlier than usual, hoping to get a head start on the day. As she drove into the city, she thought of the promise she'd made. By Friday she would decide whether or not there was a real possibility she would follow Leota to the States.

Leota had talked of the exciting changes they would make. There would be a new, larger apartment in Washington, D.C. or even a house in neighboring Virginia. Leota would pull strings to get Carol a green card and then employment in law enforcement, perhaps consulting to the FBI. And there were all the other myriad delights in travel, in culture, the United States could offer. It would be a new, shining life together.

Leota was returning to Canberra today, but would be back in time for Aunt Sarah's portrait showing.

"I'm mighty curious to meet Sybil," she'd said.

Carol had kept her tone light. "Fine for you, darling, but I'm not so sure I like the idea of you two comparing notes. You are a trained interrogator, after all."

Leota had given her soft, warm chuckle. "Nothing she can say can turn me away"—she seized Carol in a hard embrace—"from my gorgeous, irresistible Aussie woman."

Carol smiled at the memory of what followed this declaration, then sobered as she considered the decision ahead. When she was with Leota, it seemed so right to have their closeness, their love for each other, translate into a long-term future together. But when Carol was away from her, doubts rushed in to chip away at this certainty.

Last night Carol had called her son to have a chat with him about the possibility she might move to the States. She'd been concerned David would be upset at the idea, but he'd discussed the matter quite thoroughly, then said, "Mum, I can visit you, right? That would be *way* cool!"

Then she'd asked to speak with his father. Since their divorce, Justin Hart and Carol maintained a civil, but cool relationship. "Yes, Carol, what is it?"

After informing him about the possibility she might be leaving Australia, Carol said, "Off the record entirely, what can you tell me about Slessor, Slessor, Dunkling and Gold? I'm particularly interested in Ambrose Slessor."

"The firm? In general they're high-profile, very successful solicitors. Ambrose Slessor fancies himself a shaker and mover, but as the saying goes, his reach often exceeds his grasp. Off the record, Carol, I'd be reluctant to be involved in any matter where Slessor is concerned. There are quiet, but persistent rumors of deals that are not quite kosher. That's all I'll say."

When she reached the Police Centre, Miles Li met her with the news he'd located Katarina Thane. Carol smiled at him affectionately. He'd been in her team for several years, and was a more than competent officer, but he still looked young enough to be attending high school.

He handed her a colored printout. "This is the homepage for Katarina Thane's website," he said. "At the moment, she's in Honolulu at some paranormal convention. Here's the number of her hotel. In Hawaii it's late Sunday evening, but she said she'd take your call no matter what time."

While Carol waited to be connected, she looked at the printout Miles Li had given her. Katarina Thane, dressed in flowing white robes, her dark hair loose on her shoulders, smiled from what appeared to be a neo-classical grotto. Over her head were the words: *Pierce the Mysteries of the Ages via Katarina Thane's Mystic Gifts*. Carol was reading through the extravagant accolades attesting to the psychic's extraordinary achievements in extrasensory perception when Katarina Thane herself came on the line.

"I'd be lying, Inspector Ashton, if I said I wasn't expecting you to contact me." The woman had a deep, buttery voice, very appropriate, Carol thought, for her chosen line of business.

Tempted to make a crack about psychic flashes, Carol contented herself with, "Indeed, Ms. Thane?"

"*Katarina*, please. I insist. You're thinking, of course, I knew you'd call because I employed some paranormal avenue. The truth is more prosaic. Chuck Inman warned me you were likely to check with me about Eric Rule."

"He did? When was this?"

"A few days ago, before he left for Australia." She gave a husky cough. "Sorry, it's the cigarettes. I keep meaning to give them up."

"You're aware Eric Rule disappeared in the Australian desert many years ago and was never found? He's officially dead."

Carol heard the unmistakable click of a lighter, and after a moment, the long exhale of a nicotine addict enjoying the first taste of a cigarette. "Chuck gave me the details."

"Mr. Inman is claiming you told him Eric Rule is actually alive and living in Australia."

"I did confirm that, yes."

Carol frowned. There seemed to her to be a subtle emphasis on the word *confirm*. "When you say confirm," she said, "it implies you're corroborating or verifying something given to you. Is that what you mean?"

"Ah!" exclaimed Katarina, "I see you have some psychic abilities yourself."

Carol had to smile. "I don't think so."

"May I be frank, Inspector Ashton?"

"Please."

"As a sensitive at the forefront of my profession," Katarina said, "I charge top rates. For a consultation I require a fifty percent deposit well in advance, the remainder to be paid immediately the consultation concludes. I'm very strict about this, but as I've known Chuck for some time, when he said he'd forgotten his check book, I'm afraid I relaxed my rules. In short, Chuck made the first payment, and stiffed me on the second."

Carol was amused to think the psychic hadn't seen this coming, but kept her tone strictly business as she said, "Understandably, you're not pleased with Mr. Inman."

"To put it mildly. As Chuck let down his side of the bargain, I have no compunction about revealing information about the session." In the pause that followed, Carol could imagine Katarina drawing in a full lungful of smoke.

A muffled cough followed, then Katarina continued, "Whatever you may think, Inspector Ashton, I *am* a genuine psychic. I'm also a business woman. If it's obvious a client is anxious for me to say something in particular, and my link to the spirit world doesn't contradict the information, I'll say it."

Intrigued, Carol sat forward. "Chuck Inman made it clear what he wanted you to come up with regarding Eric Rule?"

"Chuck guided the whole session. He was paying—or so I

thought—so I was willing to go along with it. Inspector, I wouldn't be revealing this little professional secret if Chuck hadn't cheated me."

Indignation colored her voice as she went on, "Chuck swore he'd put a check in the mail for the outstanding amount. It never turned up. I left messages for him. No reply. Then, a few days ago, he called to say he was sorry about the problem. He'd stopped payment on the first check and was issuing a new one. And he mentioned it was very likely I'd be hearing from an Inspector Ashton of the Sydney police, and would I confirm everything that had come up in the consultation about Eric Rule being alive."

"I'd be guessing," said Carol, "but I'd say the second check hasn't arrived."

Katarina snorted. "It hasn't. If you see Chuck, tell him I'm gunning for him. Tell him he's clocking up mucho bad karma—and bad karma will get you every time."

"I'll pass that on."

"And Inspector, I don't presume to tell you your business, but I have an insight about Chuck Inman I must share with you. He lies for the sake of lying. It's a game with him. Pathological liar would be a good label for him."

After she'd thanked the psychic, Carol sat at her desk musing over Chuck Inman's reasons for concocting the story about Eric Rule. It was unlikely, but still possible that Rule's son had deliberately disappeared and had stayed out of sight for so long. Such things happened. Each year, a small but constant number of people walked out of their lives and vanished. Those who were traced gave varied reasons for their vanishing acts: overwhelming stress, leaving an unendurable relationship, ducking onerous responsibilities, simply the desire to escape a humdrum existence. A few had committed criminal acts, often embezzlement, and were running from arrest.

Eric Rule didn't seem to fit into any of these categories, but Carol knew the human heart was hard to read. Perhaps he had found the disappointed expectations of his father too great a burden to bear.

Even though the possibility he'd survived had to be considered, Carol was convinced Eric was dead, the most likely scenario being that he'd wandered away from the site and had perished from exposure.

It was still very early, but she tried Ambrose Slessor anyway. He wasn't in, so she left a message on his voicemail. She had told Ophelia Rule she would speak with Slessor, and had intended to do so, but Jim Flint's murder had pushed Slessor onto the do-later list.

She was checking the points she wanted to cover with the solicitor when Les Upton knocked on the door. Carol was beginning to pick up the subtleties of Upton's expressions, so when he appeared with the faintest of smiles, she said, "You've got something interesting to tell me, Les."

"Could be. It just so happens Kent Humphries belongs to the Eastern Suburbs Rugby League Club. Has for quite a few years. That means it's very possible he could have run into Hawkins and Doherty and co-opted them to kill Rule's daughter." With a frown, apparently at his failure, he added, "I can't find anyone else in the Rule camp who's had any contact with Hawkins or Doherty, and worse, I've come up with absolutely nothing as far as a money trail is concerned. I reckon payment to these two was strictly cash."

"Why would Humphries recruit from a club where he's a member? Isn't that practically begging us to find the connection?"

Upton tilted his head slightly. "Maybe he had no choice. When I got chatting to this guy—Boyle his name is—in the club office, it turned out he knew exactly who Humphries was. He's a fanatical supporter of the team and never misses a Roosters match when he's in Sydney. As for the club itself, Humphries has got himself fully involved—volunteers for everything going. Boyle says Humphries is a bit of sad case. No real friends, and not much of a life outside football."

"That could describe any number of men I know," said Carol with a grin.

"And I've got more." With a gesture that for Upton was close to a flourish, he put a sheet of paper in front of her. "Here's Chuck Inman's travel schedule as far as Australia's concerned."

Carol's eyebrows rose. "Inman's been here three times?" She rested her chin on her hand. "And he very carefully led me to believe he'd never set foot in Australia."

"Probably banking on the fact no one would bother checking." Upton indicated the top entry on the sheet. "See this first visit to Sydney? Fascinating to know it's two months, almost to the day, before the boating accident that killed the Webbs. He stayed in Sydney two weeks, then went back to Texas."

"Did he visit South Australia when he was here?"

"Couldn't find any trace he did, but that doesn't mean much."

Carol sat back to regard Upton. "So what are you thinking, Les?"

"That it's possible Inman came here to oversee the arrangements to blow up the Webb family, then beat it before it happened."

"The timing could be a coincidence."

Upton grunted. "Yeah? Then how come he timed his second visit to Sydney two weeks before Martina Rule got hers in the parking lot. He was sightseeing at the Great Barrier Reef the day she died."

"What airline does Inman use?"

"Not Qantas, if you're thinking he met up with Kent Humphries. United Airlines every time, including this third visit. There must be something here that's pulling him back, wouldn't you say?" His lips twitched. "Money is the root of all evil," he intoned.

Anne Newsome, entering, announced, "It's the *love* of money that's the root of all evil, Les, not the money itself."

Carol said, "Les has discovered this is Chuck Inman's third visit to Australia. Although it's no evidence worth anything by itself, he timed his first two visits rather curiously. The first was a couple of months before the Webbs died, the second around the time Martina Rule was killed."

121

"Makes you wonder," said Upton, "who wins the booby prize this visit."

"The heirs are getting thin on the ground," said Anne with a grin.

"He's careful to have an alibi, so someone has to do his dirty work for him," said Upton. "My pick is Humphries. He was here when Stewart died, and again when Flint was murdered. And he was in the States when Fancee Porter wiped herself out."

Thinking perhaps her initial pessimism about Upton's usefulness in the team might have been unjustified, Carol was about to speak, when Upton accurately reflected her thoughts with, "Now you'll be wanting me to check where Humphries was when the Webbs and the Rule girl cashed it in. Right?"

"Right. And one more thing. Both Ian Stewart and Ophelia Rule got detailed family trees anonymously mailed to them. Kent Humphries says he didn't. I want to know whether Jim Flint and Rosalie Webb received this helpful family tree mailing too. Don't worry about including Chuck Inman. I intend to see him myself."

When Upton had gone, Anne said, "About Stewart's signature on his suicide note, I've got an expert opinion."

"Inconclusive? There are only three letters in *Ian*."

"Inconclusive. But she did say, if pushed, she'd be inclined to say Stewart hadn't signed the note."

"It's one brick in the wall, and we need a lot more. I'm going to advise the Coroner's Court we're requesting a delay on Stewart's inquest. Now, Anne, how about Ledmark?"

"I had a friendly drink with Dave Ledmark last night. It seems Fred Verrell's been giving Dave and one of the other security guys, Sam Gallagher, quite a bit of part-time work. Their job at the Rule estate isn't very demanding these days, being more like glorified caretaking, so they both moonlight as security at rock concerts, act as bodyguards for various celebrities and so on. In Inman's case, Dave and Sam split the time between them, but at the most, so far it's only been a few hours."

"Inman doesn't want cover twenty-four hours a day?"

"Only when he leaves the hotel. And Dave says Inman doesn't behave in the slightest as if he believes he's in any danger."

"So why the bodyguard?" Carol asked.

"For show? To give himself an alibi at a crucial time?"

"Good point," said Carol. "I've already told Ophelia to make sure her brother's security is enhanced, because the way he is, he's a sitting duck. I'll call and remind her that she needs added security too, and the same for Kent Humphries. Mark's advised Ricky Webb's guardians there may be danger, and they've moved him to a secret address. And I suppose I'd better warn Inman, bodyguard or no bodyguard."

"I figure someone on the list doesn't need a warning, because he's the killer."

"We may be leaping to conclusions here, Anne. Perhaps there's something we need to know."

Anne smiled. "Like Eric Rule is alive? Do you really think so?"

"No, but stranger things have happened."

The phone rang. It was Slessor's assistant returning Carol's call. "Inspector Ashton, Mr. Slessor really has very little time today. He's due in court with Hubert Fox shortly." Hubert Fox was an eminent barrister, and Carol was sure the assistant had emphasized the name to let her know how relatively unimportant Carol's request was.

"I have one quick matter to discuss with him."

Silence, then a displeased, "Very well. I'll get Mr. Slessor for you."

Slessor came on the line almost immediately. "Inspector Ashton? What's the question? You understand, I'm a little rushed this morning."

Carol was direct. "Apart from his doctors, who knew Thurmond Rule was dying, and when did they know it?"

"I'm not sure I can answer that."

Carol imagined his pencil-thin mustache twitching. She said, "When did *you* learn the news, Mr. Slessor?"

"I . . . Indeed, I'm not altogether sure. In the last months it was obvious Rule was a very sick man. He, himself, of course, was in complete denial. I do recall Dr. McMinn talking with me, but as for the precise date . . ."

"Was it before Rule's daughter died?"

"It may have been."

With what Carol thought of as typical lawyers' caution, Slessor was failing to commit himself to any hard facts. She said, "Did you tell anyone else?"

"That he was dying? Certainly not the media. I believe I discussed it with Juanita Paz, but obviously in her nursing role, she was already aware of the prognosis."

"What about people outside the household? Did you mention it to one of your partners, perhaps?"

"Naturally not. I wouldn't discuss such matters."

Carol didn't believe him. It would be natural, she thought, to share with trusted colleagues the fact that one of the most powerful and hated businessmen in the country was about to shuffle off the mortal coil.

"Inspector? I really must finish this call."

"Mr. Slessor, do you own shares in any of Thurmond Rule's companies?"

"I beg your pardon?"

When Carol repeated her question, Slessor's voice swelled with indignation. "Are you implying something improper?"

"Not at all. A routine question."

"I have no intention of discussing my personal financial details with you, Inspector. Good day to you!"

Replacing the receiver, Carol smiled to herself. She had certainly ruffled the solicitor's feathers. She called Mark Bourke in, recounted the conversation she'd just had, and said, "What do you think? There could be financial motives quite outside the billions in the Rule estate. Knowledge of Rule's fatal illness and imminent demise could affect the stock market materially, I imagine."

"I'm onto it," said Mark. "Nothing I like more than to find out how much more money everyone else has than I do."

• • •

The information the Stewart inquest had been delayed resulted in a plethora of calls from the media. Anything even seemingly peripheral to the Rule inheritance was scoring high on media radar. Chuck Inman's name was mentioned many times. It became apparent he was not only talking up his Eric Rule scenario, but other hypotheses as well, including what he referred to as "the possibility of a rogue killer heir." Naturally, he made much of his need for a bodyguard, painting himself as the one innocent in the whole affair, and also managed some slyly oblique references to the inefficiency of the police in the matter. Inman was, Carol thought, a one-man rumor machine, running at full bore.

In between calls from the media, Carol contacted Kent Humphries to advise him to take extra care—he reacted with alarm—and then Ophelia with the same message.

"Oh, for God's sake!" Ophelia snapped. "I can bloody take care of myself. I'd like to see the bastard who could take me down."

Privately agreeing it was likely to take someone extraordinary to subdue the woman, Carol contrasted that somewhat amusing thought with the plight of Nicholas Jordan. "And you did arrange for tightened security for your brother, didn't you?"

"Yeah, yeah." Ophelia terminated the call without saying goodbye.

Bourke came in while Carol was watering her plant. "Too much water," he observed, "is as bad, if not worse, than not enough."

"Thanks for your horticultural advice."

"I've got other information you might like to hear. The details of Chuck Inman's various, and often wondrous, business activities have come through. He's been involved in a whole range of questionable companies and partnerships, but nothing that's landed him in the slammer. My favorite is his attempt to start a church cum charity organization he called Deity Dollars. He and his erstwhile partner,

125

Chip O'Hanna—who has, incidentally, served time—were selling the concept of buying your way into heaven to mainly poor and/or retired people. A rival telemarketing evangelist blew the whistle on them, and Deity Dollars went out of business before it could really get going."

"Any suggestion of violence in Inman's history?"

"No, he's a scam artist more than anything else."

Bourke walked over to examine the whiteboard on which the Rule heirs were listed. "You know," he said, "I think we can write Fancee Porter's death off as an accident. I've looked at the police reports again, and there's not the slightest suggestion anyone spiked her drink, or ran her off the road. I think it's a coincidence that her death seems linked to the others."

Upton had come into Carol's office while Bourke was talking. "You might like to change your mind when you hear Kent Humphries has been free and unaccounted for in every case, including being available to blow up the Webbs, and also to organize Martina Rule's death." His satisfaction clear, he went on, "I've checked with Qantas, and he wasn't in a cabin crew either time. He's our boy, I'm sure of it."

"He could have an alibi for some of them, Les," Carol said.

"Maybe, but I think it's more than odd Humphries just happened to visit this Fancee Porter just before she died."

"The odd thing is," Carol said, "he's always available."

Bourke stood looking at the list, rubbing the side of his jaw reflectively. "Fall guy?" he said to Carol.

"It's worth a thought."

Upton puckered his brow just sufficiently to indicate his opposition to this idea. "Too hard to do. Think of the logistics of setting Humphries up. You'd have to time everything just so. Hey, you have to have the guy followed, twenty-four hours a day. Who could be doing that?"

Bourke said, "Someone with security training, a private eye . . ." He looked at Carol. "Fred Verrell?"

"Two minds," said Carol, "with but a single thought."

• • •

Verrell had offices in Darlinghurst, not far from the Police Centre. Carol and Bourke entered to find the receptionist's desk unattended. The sound of a querulous voice in a nearby office pinpointed Fred Verrell's location. He didn't hide his displeasure when they appeared at the office door. "I don't believe you have an appointment," he snapped, scooping up his little black poodle, Nero, and putting him under one arm. His action was a source of relief to Carol, as Nero had been eyeing her ankle with bared teeth.

Verrell raised his voice to bellow, "Barbara, where the fucking hell are you? You supposed to stop the riffraff getting to me!"

"Sorry," came faintly from the outer office. Verrell swore under his breath.

"Miniature poodle, is he?" said Bourke pleasantly, indicating Nero.

Verrell made a disgusted sound. "*Toy* poodle, if you must know. Now, let's skip the chitchat. What do you want?" He retreated to the far side of his desk to glare at them. Carol suspected this move was to avoid having the disparity between his height and Mark Bourke's made obvious.

"You're supplying bodyguards for Mr. Inman."

"So? It's not a secret, Inspector."

"Have you provided professional services for any of the other Rule heirs?" Bourke asked.

He began to list the names, but Verrell made an impatient gesture. "I'm not a fool. I know who they are. The answer's no. Now, if you don't mind, I'm a busy man."

Carol said, "Kent Humphries."

There was the slightest change of expression on Verrell's face before he said, "What about him? He works for Qantas. He's a claimant. That's all I know. One of my men, Patterson, checked him out for Slessor when Humphries came forward as a would-be heir."

"So you've never met Mr. Humphries?" Bourke said.

Verrell shrugged. "Never, to my knowledge. Why?"

Carol said, "Could you check your records? We have reliable information suggesting Kent Humphries has been under surveillance by your company over some period of time."

Nero gave a protesting yelp, then glared at his master. Verrell said, "I don't need to check anything. No operative of mine has ever followed Humphries anywhere, anytime."

"Perhaps you did the job yourself," said Bourke.

"I'm not going to keep denying something that never happened. Please leave."

"Would you mind giving us the names of those who work for you, both full and part-time?" Carol asked.

Verrell bounced to his feet. "Not without a court order. Now, get out!"

As they left, Barbara in the reception area gave them a sullen glance. She was young, waifish, and a bleached blonde. "Barbara, get in here!" was yelled from Verrell's office as they closed the door.

Outside in the sunshine, Bourke said with a grin, "Smooth, Carol, slipping in that `reliable information` we have on Humphries being followed."

"Worth it to see the poodle squeeze test. A living lie detector, wouldn't you say?"

"No way would Verrell have followed Humphries himself," said Bourke. "He could have used several people, or been smart, and kept it to one. We need some names."

"We can get them, but it'll take time."

"Fortunately," said Bourke, "loose lips can always be found. I wonder who could charm the delightful Barbara best? Miles or Les? Or maybe Anne can do the 'girls together against the world' routine . . ."

● ● ●

Mid-afternoon Carol received a call from Madeline Shipley. "Carol, darling, such a long time since we've spoken, or, indeed, done anything interesting together." She gave her husky, suggestive laugh. "Perhaps for old times sake we could meet?"

Madeline's *Shipley Report* had for many years now been a consistently high-rating program, specializing in providing background to news items of particular interest to the general public. Carol sometimes watched, marveling at how Madeline's polished beauty never seemed to change. It seemed unfair, when Carol's mirror unkindly informed Carol she was definitely getting older.

"I'll take a rain check, Madeline. How can I help you?"

"Chuck Inman. He's spinning quite a tale of murder and mayhem. Our lawyers are looking at the tape very closely. We've had to edit out a lot, but it's still a sensational story. I wonder if I could get a comment, Carol, on or off the record."

Carol sat back in her chair and thought. After a moment she said, "On the record—we've met with Mr. Inman, and hope to meet with him again."

"That's it?"

Knowing she could trust Madeline, at least on a professional level, Carol said, "Off the record now, okay?"

"Very okay. What've you got for me?"

"Chuck Inman's not that far from the truth with his reference to a rogue killer heir. His terminology is amusing, but the situation isn't. I believe we do have a serial killer here, Madeline. Someone has, conservatively, killed five people, possibly six if you count Fancee Porter in the States, although she may be the only true accident in the bunch."

"Carol! This is dynamite!"

"You can't use it yet, but I'll give you an exclusive if you give me a favor in return."

"Sold," said Madeline.

CHAPTER ELEVEN

The week passed quickly. Carol called Juanita Paz. Hector Paz answered the phone. "My wife? Why do you want to speak with her?"

"I have a further question about her nursing of Mr. Rule."

"I can answer anything you want to know."

It took several minutes of Carol's patient persistence before Juanita's hesitant voice came on the line. "I've told you everything I know, Inspector Ashton."

Thinking that Hector Paz was almost certainly listening in on another handset, Carol said, "How long before his death did you learn that Mr. Rule was going to die?"

"I'm not sure . . ."

"Pancreatic cancer is very often fatal, isn't it? When you heard the diagnosis, you must have realized your patient might not survive his illness for too long. Approximately what date would this be?"

Silence. Then Juanita said in her soft, ineffectual voice, "I'm not sure. A few months, I think."

"Not more than that? Not, for instance, eight months? Ten?"

"Oh, no, not as long as that." Juanita rallied to add in a more positive voice, "I always think the most positive thoughts where my patients are concerned. I don't consider death at all, most of the time, so I can't answer your question, Inspector Ashton."

Carol tapped her gold pen on her desk. Juanita Paz, she decided, was going to give deliberately fuzzy answers to anything she was asked. Carol said, "Did you discuss the fact Mr. Rule had a fatal illness with anyone else?"

"I'm not sure what you're getting at."

Carol repeated the question.

Juanita paused, then said, "With Dr. McMinn, of course. And perhaps some of the other medical staff who came to see Mr. Rule . . ."

"Anyone outside?"

"I don't know what you mean."

This was like trying to grab smoke. Carol hid her impatience, saying, "Did you mention to anyone outside the household that Thurmond Rule was going to die?"

"Of course not! I don't think anyone here would do such a thing."

After Carol had hung up, she sat staring into space. Anne had said to her that Dave Ledmark had described a very different Juanita Paz, a woman who had a strong influence on the wild Martina Rule. On an impulse, she called Canberra, and got Leota on the line. "This is business, not pleasure, darling. I need some information on two Colombians . . ."

She called Anne in. "Hector and Juanita Paz came to Australia about thirteen years ago. I want you to see what you can dig up in Colombia. It could be interesting to know their history before they came here."

She passed a slip of paper to Anne. "This guy's CIA. Leota's contacting him to say you'll be calling. He's been involved in Colombia for the last twenty years. If there's anything there, he'll find it."

On Thursday morning Carol had a long, trying meeting with the Commissioner. Superintendent Edgar, who'd been excluded, despite his best efforts, waylaid her on her way back to her office. "So what's happening, Carol?"

"The Commissioner's agreed to have Chuck Inman watched twenty-four hours a day. It's unlikely he'll do anything incriminating, but he's our best bet at the moment."

This wasn't enough for Edgar. He insisted that Carol should go through the meeting item by item. "The Commissioner would want me in the loop," he declared.

Only one thing made Edgar's officiousness bearable. Although she didn't say anything to him about this, at the close of the meeting the Commissioner had said to her, "I've been looking at your record, Carol. It's an excellent one, except for one serious slip. It seems to me you should have been promoted long ago. If you bring this case to a satisfactory conclusion, I can't imagine anything will stand in your way to becoming Chief Detective Inspector Ashton."

Late on Thursday Bourke reported on the solicitor's financial dealings. "The Fraud Squad's up to their eyes in it, but I managed to get some background stuff on Slessor, Slessor, Dunkling and Gold, and more particularly on Ambrose Slessor."

"As far as the public's concerned," said Carol, "this firm of solicitors is right at the top of the profession."

"No one's suggested the partners aren't sharp," said Bourke, "but Kent Humphries was right to be wary. My man in Fraud says there've been some deals that came awfully close to ethics violations. It was all kept in the legal family though, and nothing leaked out. The legal watchdogs have had their eyes on Ambrose Slessor in particular, but although there have been some questionable deals, in a couple of cases with the administration of large estates, nothing's been blatant enough to get any action."

"What's your take on it, Mark?"

"Slessor bends the rules, but never breaks them. He has a very expensive lifestyle, an extremely expensive trophy wife, and two spoilt kids who expect the world on a stick. I'd say if there was a way to safely tap the Rule billions, he'd leap at it."

"Let's say," said Carol, "I come to Ambrose Slessor as a valid heir. I don't mention it, but I've already disposed of Rosalie Webb and then Martina Rule, in order to move up in the inheritance stakes. I tell Slessor I don't like the idea of sharing with seven others. In return for his professional help, I'd be very generous to him, however. Now, before the court determines who gets what, Slessor and I set out to thin the field dramatically."

"It could work," said Bourke. "The money's certainly tempting enough, and Slessor's had sticky fingers in the past. But which heir? Humphries? The fair Ophelia? Chuck Inman?"

"Perhaps Kent Humphries is smart enough to set himself up as a fall guy, so he can ultimately accuse someone else of deliberately implicating him."

"I like Ophelia," said Bourke. He added, laughing, "But then, I'm always attracted to strong women."

"Chuck Inman," said Carol, "is featured on *The Shipley Report* tonight. I know he'll never be able to resist seeing himself on the screen, so let's see if he's at his hotel. Perhaps we can drop in and share the moment."

"Let me check," said Bourke. A quick call gave the information he required. "He's in his hotel suite. He's ordered a call girl for nine o'clock, no expenses spared. It'd be unkind if we stayed too late, don't you think?"

• • •

Inman had a suite in a luxury hotel near Circular Quay. Although Carol and Bourke arrived unannounced, he seemed quite happy to wave them through the door. Today he was wearing ancient brown trousers and a T-shirt proclaiming *The Lone Star State . . . Texas*

Forever! His feet were bare. Carol noted he'd shaved, but his long, reddish hair still seemed innocent of a brush.

The suite was large and well-appointed. On the bar a bottle of champagne sat in ice. Indicating the two champagne flutes, Carol said, "We're interrupting something?"

Inman sent a conspiratorial grin in Bourke's direction. "We men always crave a little female company, if you see what I mean."

Carol introduced Mark Bourke. Pumping Bourke's hand, Inman said, "Call me Chuck." He waved them to chairs, and took a seat himself. "Found Eric Rule yet?" he asked.

"I wonder you can say that with a straight face, Mr. Inman."

Chuck Inman looked suitably injured. "I do wonder what you mean by that, Inspector Ashton."

"I've spoken to Katarina Thane."

"And she confirms, I'm sure, everything I've been saying. That young woman has a link to the great unknown, the parallel universe, the sixth sense . . . whatever you care to call it."

Bourke grinned. "So you believe everything this psychic says?"

Sincerity flowing from him, Inman said, "I do. I really do."

Carol smiled in turn. "I have a message for you from Ms. Thane. She said to tell you she hadn't received your second check, and you are accumulating bad karma at quite a rate."

Inman dismissed this with a click of his tongue. "Katarina can get carried away at times. The check's in the mail, as they say."

"Ms. Thane stated quite categorically that you fed the story about Eric Rule to her, and she obligingly gave it back to you in the form you could use—the apparent revelations of a psychic."

Unperturbed, Inman asked, "Why would I bother to do that?"

"We've been wondering that too," said Bourke. "To stir up trouble? Confuse us poor cops with a false lead? Inflame the media? Or my personal favorite—because it's fun to do."

Carol was about to mention Madeline Shipley's program when Inman obligingly checked his watch. "Speaking of the media," he said, "there's an item I don't want to miss on a show starting right about now."

He grabbed the remote from a table near his chair and clicked on the TV. Madeline Shipley's smooth voice welcomed everyone to *The Shipley Report*.

At that moment, the phone rang. Inman made an exasperated sound as he snatched up the receiver. "Yes?" Carol saw his shoulders tighten. "Can't talk now. I'm not alone. Yes, okay."

On the screen, an ad for toothpaste was playing. Inman, looking artificially casual, replaced the handset. Carol was betting he wouldn't take the best course, which was to say nothing about the call, but that he would try some explanation. She was right.

"I'm in the way of becoming a media star," he said with a self-deprecating laugh. "These journalists, they can get you anywhere."

Carol didn't respond, nor did Bourke. Inman cleared his throat, adjusted the volume of the set even louder than before, and waited for the advertisements to end. After blandishments to buy insurance, petrol, a new watering system and a toilet cleaner, Madeline reappeared to do the introduction of the first story.

"It's me," said Inman, now quite relaxed that his image was on. Madeline did her usual excellent job. She was an assured interviewer, not pushy, but relentless in the most charming way. Chuck Inman had a good persona for television, Carol thought. He projected a type of rugged, untidy individualism—a man who marched to his own tune. And Carol had to admit he seemed convincing enough, no matter how bizarre his basic theories seemed to be.

The interview had obviously been tightly edited, and with Australia's draconian libel laws in mind, Inman wasn't permitted to directly accuse anyone. It was all generalities, but couched in a heartfelt manner. Carol almost found herself believing him.

At the wrap-up, Madeline came through for Carol with the material they'd discussed earlier in the week. In a close-up on her almost flawless face, she said, "You have heard Mr. Inman's fascinating, disturbing story of inheritance and mysterious death, of psychics and bodies in the desert. *The Shipley Report* is proud to announce we are in a position to break stunning new developments in this matter. Hard evidence of premeditated murder, of conspiracy, of many months of lethal planning, of the destruction of a family with almost unbelievable savagery. Of the deliberate framing of an innocent party." She paused, looking deep into the camera. "More revelations after these important messages."

Another slew of ads began. Inman gave an anxious laugh. "She's got a scoop, she says. Of course, you'd know all about that. So what gives?"

Bourke said, his tone portentous, "We can't comment, Mr. Inman."

"Off the record, then. I won't be saying anything to anyone."

Carol smile cynically. "Like you weren't saying anything in the program we've just watched?"

More advertisements, then a promo for a new show. Madeline was back, as polished as a living work of art. She gave a brief précis of the points she'd already made, then finished with, "As soon as we're able, we will present to you the whole shocking, wicked story of greed and death. Arrests are pending. The moment we are free to do so, we will present the facts, in all their appalling truth."

After they left Chuck Inman, who Carol thought was doing a good job of hiding his growing alarm, Bourke checked the technicians conducting the phone tap.

"A whispered voice," he relayed to Carol. "Said Inman's name, he responded as we heard at our end, then the caller said there'd be another contact later. The call was too short to trace."

"Let's see if Chuck's alarmed enough to call back."

● ● ●

The next day Miles Li, rolling his eyes, gave Carol the list of Verrell's staff he'd used sweet persuasion to get from Barbara, Verrell's receptionist. "She's rough," he said with what Carol took to be masterly understatement. She put Miles onto checking out each name, but she didn't have much hope it would lead to anything, as she suspected Verrell would use a free-lancer whose name wouldn't appear on his books.

Maureen Oatland came bouncing in as Carol was packing up early so she'd have time to pick up her son and take him with her to Sybil's place for the portrait showing.

"I've hit pay dirt, Carol! Remember I left my business cards at the pub in case I missed anyone who might have seen Flint leave with someone? Well, I've just had a call from a guy called Billy Murdoch, who says he saw Jim Flint that night with a woman. I'm on my way to the *Quitters' Arms* to interview him right now."

"Once you talk with him, call me on my mobile, Maureen."

"Will do."

Maureen bustled off, radiating cheerful self-assurance. There was something about Maureen's good-humored vitality that inspired even reluctant witnesses to talk. Carol had no doubt if there was information to be gained, Maureen was the one to extract it.

Carol's son, David, lived with his father and stepmother in the eastern suburbs. He'd wrangled an invitation to the portrait show-ing, partly because he'd known Sybil for years and was very fond of her, but mainly because Aunt Sarah had promised Eco-Crone Lillian Broadhall would give him all the gruesome details about being arrested and thrown into a Thai jail.

Carol picked him up after work, and drove directly to the north-ern beaches via the Sydney Harbour Bridge. David didn't mention the possibility of Carol going to the States, but chattered away about his new school, about sports, about the hair-raising exploits of one of his friends, then asked Carol about the Rule case.

"Darling," said Carol, "you know I can't tell you anything."

"Ah, jeez! Just something, Mum. I told the guys you were way cool."

"Way cool will get you nowhere," Carol laughed. "Just what have you promised?"

"Like, stuff that isn't on TV. That guy who got his throat cut—what he looked like. The blood, and stuff."

"Sorry. No can do." Carol looked over affectionately at her lanky son. He seemed to be growing taller at an incredible rate. Any day now, he'd look down on her.

"Then I'll have to make it up." He gave her an inveigling grin. "It'd be much better if you just told me, Mum."

Carol drew up at Sybil's driveway. "Out you get. I'll park the car." She felt a tug at her heart as he bounded up the steps to the front door. Too soon he'd be a man, swaggering with the confidence of youth out into the world. He'd have girlfriends—or, she reminded herself, perhaps boyfriends.

She smiled as she walked back down the hill from the parking spot she'd finally found. Seeing David suddenly spurt from childhood into a young man had shaken her a little. It was hard to conceive, but hell! one day she could become a grandmother . . .

Pausing outside in the driveway, she looked up at the house. The buzz of conversation poured from the open windows. Somebody laughed uproariously. Leota should be here already. She'd called on her drive up from Canberra saying she was making good time, and would meet Carol at the party.

All week Carol had wrestled with the decision she was to give to Leota tonight. She'd vacillated, argued with herself, considered every option. She'd changed her mind so many times she should be dizzy. But now she was going in to find Leota and say, *Yes, I'll follow you to the States. I cannot bear to lose what we have together.*

Sybil's spacious house was crammed with people, all busily eating, drinking, talking. Aunt Sarah's portrait, subtly floodlit, hung on a wall by itself. Carol waved to several Eco-Crones she knew as she made her way over for a closer look. Yancey Blake, wearing black pants, a heavy gold tunic and huge dangling jade earrings, came up to Carol as she surveyed it.

"What do you think?" Yancey asked.

Displayed like this, the painting seemed so much more impressive than when Carol had seen it unframed. The image of Aunt Sarah glowed almost incandescently. Yancey had not idealized her, but equally, she had paid her subject due respect. Humor and intelligence shone in her aunt's eyes, and Carol had a sense of the passion for the environment that had led her to become an activist. Warmth

138

spilled from her upright, somehow heroic figure, to embrace the creatures crowding behind her on the canvas.

"It's terrific," Carol said with total sincerity. "You've painted a wonderful portrait. Aunt Sarah must be so pleased."

Someone came to gush to Yancey about art, and Carol drifted away in search of Leota. She snagged a glass of red wine and a wedge of cheese, and began a determined scan of the crowd.

Lillian Broadhall, gracefully angular, said to her, "Still catching villains?"

"I try."

"Good." Lillian jerked her gray head in the direction of the painting. "Sarah's portrait—what do you think?" she said in her customary laconic manner.

"It's hard to capture my aunt on canvas, but I think Yancey's done it."

"Her free spirit. Yes." Lillian caught Carol's elbow, leaned closer to her, said, "Wanting to see you. Ambrose Slessor? He's here, you know. Yancey Blake's painting his portrait. Vain man. Very vain."

"You know him?"

"Unfortunately, yes. My dear friend, Rose, was married to a man who fancied himself a business whiz. Bad mistake. Her late husband was in partnership at one point with Ambrose Slessor. Ted had big ideas, not much gray matter. Total failure. Two, three hundred thousand down the gurgler. Rose and he nearly lost the house. And Ambrose Slessor? No problems for him." She fixed Carol with a narrow-eyed stare. "Crooked as a dog's hind leg."

"Was there any legal action after the business failure?"

"No. Ambrose is sharp as a tack. What I'm saying is, anything he's mixed up with . . ." She turned her thumb down in an expressive gesture. "Everyone loses, except Ambrose. Big bobbly head. Huge ambitions. No morality. He's involved in this Thurmond Rule thing? Bad news for everyone but Ambrose."

Aunt Sarah, beaming, appeared with David in tow. "Here's Lillian," she said to him.

139

"Is it true you were in a Thai prison?"

"Horrible place. You wouldn't want to be there." Lillian grinned at him. "Want the grisly details?"

"Yes, please."

Leaving David and Lillian Broadhall deep in conversation, Aunt Sarah led Carol in the direction of the kitchen. "Leota's in there, talking with Sybil," she said with a sideways look.

"That's nice."

Her aunt grinned. "Isn't it?"

Ambrose Slessor, naturally wearing a well-tailored dark suit, nodded his pendulous head in acknowldgement as she passed him. His expression, Carol noted with ironic amusement, was sour. It was clear she was persona non grata as far as he was concerned.

Mark Bourke blocked her way. "Carol, can I see you for a moment?"

"I'll tell Leota you're here," said Aunt Sarah. She patted Bourke affectionately on the arm as she passed him. "Where's Pat?"

"My better half's in the kitchen, with Leota and Sybil. Probably hatching some dangerous scheme. I suspect they're plotting to join your Eco-Crones as a junior branch."

Aunt Sarah went off cackling.

"What is it, Mark?"

"You'd already left when Anne got the information from Leota's CIA contact. Hector and Juanita Paz—they were involved in a suspicious death thirteen years ago." He gave a grim smile. "See if you find this cast familiar. We have an attentive personal assistant. We have a very sweet, caring nurse. We have a rich man, very ill."

"Let me guess. The rich man dies."

"Yes, unexpectedly. Sums of money are unaccounted for. The family points accusing fingers. The assistant and nurse are predictably horrified at the allegations."

"There was an investigation?"

"Yes, of the brother and sister."

"Brother and sister?"

140

Bourke grinned. "They're not married, at least not legally. Hector and Juanita are brother and sister. Family name is Valencia. Their papers are excellent forgeries, good enough to get them into Australia, and good enough to fool Thurmond Rule's screening before he hired them."

Carol remembered her idle thought that the two looked almost like brother and sister. "Are they wanted in Colombia?"

"Not for killing the old guy, no. The investigation came up with nothing but suspicions. Total lack of hard evidence. The family, however, persisted, and they had money enough to keep it up until something broke. No doubt to escape the heat, the name Valencia became Paz, and Hector and Juanita became husband and wife. They left Colombia for the fresh fields of Australia."

"Here you are!" Leota put an arm around Carol's waist and squeezed her gently. "I've missed you, honey."

"Darling, I'm sorry, I'll be a moment."

Leota smiled. "No problem. I'll freshen your drink." She took Carol's glass and headed off toward the knot of people around the bar.

"Things are coming together," Carol said to Bourke. She told him about Maureen Oatland's possible witness. "She'll call as soon as she has anything."

Pat claimed Bourke and took him away to meet the infamous Hazel Foster with the Eco-Crone record in arrests at demonstrations.

"Carol?"

Carol turned at Sybil's familiar voice. "Hi. Great party."

Sybil was wearing a simple green dress of just the shade to make her red hair flame with life. "I ran into Leota in the kitchen, we introduced ourselves. Got talking."

Carol felt a tremor of tension. "Yes . . . ?"

"She's really nice, Carol." A pause. "She says she's returning to the States."

A cautious nod seemed to Carol to be the best response. Not

141

understanding why she suddenly felt so apprehensive, she said, "Leota was never going to live here permanently."

Watching her closely, Sybil said, "Are you going too?"

"Yes." It was as if she'd struck Sybil's face. Seeing her flinch, Carol heard herself say, "No . . . I'm not sure . . ."

Her phone chirped. It must be Maureen. She seized it as an escape from a conversation that had suddenly become a minefield. "Carol Ashton." As she listened, the noise of the party faded into the far background. She asked a few quick questions, gave some instructions, said, "I'll be there—half an hour, forty minutes," and terminated the call.

"I have to go," she said to Sybil. "Sorry to leave so early. I drove David here—"

"I'll look after David."

Catching sight of Bourke's head above the throng, she beckoned him over with an urgent gesture. "Mark, Nicholas Jordan's been found dead in his bed. Crime scene are on the way. And just as a precaution, I'm having Kent Humphries picked up."

"I'll come with you," said Bourke. "Pat can take our car."

"I've got to find Leota."

"Present and accounted for," Leota said from behind her. "You've got an emergency?"

"Yes, I'm sorry, but I've got to go."

"Hey," said Leota, "if there's one thing I understand, it's your job, Carol. I'll be waiting for you at home, okay?" She leaned forward to whisper, "However late you are, wake me. I've got a few new moves I've been perfecting."

142

CHAPTER TWELVE

Ophelia Rule was hysterical in the grand, dramatic understanding of the word. "I killed him! I killed my only brother!" she shrieked.

"I've given her something," said the harried head doctor, who'd been called from home, "but it doesn't seem to have had much effect."

"Does she often visit her brother?"

He snorted down his long nose. "Not likely. She pays the bills, questions every expense, and if we're lucky, drops by every six months or so."

"I understand she requested additional security for her brother."

"First I've heard of it."

Carol was turning away when she thought of another question. "Doctor, what was Jordan's long-term prognosis?"

"He had brain damage of course, and was in a coma, but it was a light one, and he had periods of almost consciousness. Breathing on his own, but otherwise totally dependent on our care."

"So there was no machine to warn he'd stopped breathing?"

"No. Our staff look in on each patient in rotation. The nurse saw immediately something was wrong, and raised the alarm."

"So without intervention, Mr. Jordan wasn't likely to die any time soon?"

The doctor grimaced. "Strong as an ox, basically. Live to be a hundred if an infection didn't carry him off. You understand, we try our best to rehabilitate our patients. It's the ones like Jordan who are money pits to their families, with no hope of ever having a meaningful life."

The long-term nursing facility was obviously well-run, but sheer economics limited the number of staff available at night. Carol had had the entire second floor sealed off, and Liz Carey, vastly irritated at having her Friday evening disturbed, was in the room with her team and the body of Nicholas Jordan. His sister had been persuaded to sit in a small waiting room, although she leapt to her feet every few minutes to wring her hands.

While Bourke organized a canvass of patients and staff, Carol took Anne with her to deal with Ophelia. Carol, by now thoroughly fed up with the histrionics, said firmly to the wailing woman, "I need you to calm down. Now. It's necessary to find out what you know."

"I know I killed him," Ophelia announced, considerably quieter. Carol would have liked to take credit for this but suspected whatever the doctor had given her was finally working.

"You didn't ask for additional security," said Carol, "but you told me you had. Why was that?"

The usual Ophelia was rapidly gaining control. She glowered at

Carol. "I didn't think it was necessary. It cost, you know. Money down the drain."

"This is Constable Newsome. She'll be asking you some questions. Please tell her everything you said or did this evening."

In the room, Liz had lights set up to illuminate the bed and victim. "No mystery about this one," she said, indicating a pillow on the floor. "Wet with his saliva. He was smothered."

"Would it take much force?"

"Carol, be serious. The guy was in a coma. A toddler could have killed him."

An hour later, Bourke and Carol had a conference together in the downstairs staff room. "Anyone could get in or out. Security's fine for drugs, but as for staff, anyone in a uniform could walk in."

Carol had turned her phone to vibrate to avoid disturbing patients disturbed enough by all the activity. When it vibrated in her pocket, she thought immediately of Maureen. It was, however, Les Upton. "Humphries has done a runner," he said. "Got his name and description out." He added, with a hint of I-told-you-so, "I guess this makes him the one, eh?"

While she was telling Bourke, her phone vibrated a second time. Maureen Oatland sounded exultant. "Murdoch came through big time, Carol. He kept quiet up to now because at the key time he was having it off in the hotel car park with a girlfriend in his van. Understandably, he didn't fancy his wife finding out. Had a change of heart." She snickered. "Asked if there was a reward, actually."

"What did he see?"

"Flint, who he knew and disliked, getting into his red truck with an older woman. Slightly built, black hair. And get this, Flint was big-noting himself that night. Boasted about this foreign woman who was hot for him."

"Juanita Paz."

"Sure sounds that way," said Maureen.

Carol found Bourke putting his own phone away. "The detail on Inman reporting in," he said. "Chuck's cracked and called. He was

145

bright enough to go down and use one of the hotel's public phones, not that it helped him, since we had them covered too. Called Hector Paz. Paz tried to calm him down, but Inman's not having any of it. Went out, hailed a cab. It looks like he's on his way to the Rule estate as we speak. The detail's covering him by car, but I've told them to keep back."

"Maureen's got a witness who's described someone very like Juanita with Flint the night he died."

"Let's go get 'em," said Bourke, usually the most circumspect of officers. "Carol?"

Carol felt a reckless heat fill her. The thrill of the chase, she thought. Or maybe it was a reaction to the frustrations, the decisions that had dogged her all the week. "You're on, Mark. I'll call Maureen back, get her over here to assist Anne. Then, let's go."

● ● ●

The unmarked police car was parked along the street from the estate's imposing gates. Carol and Bourke stopped to confer with the plain clothes officers inside. "Inman arrived about forty minutes ago," said the driver. "Paid off the taxi and talked to the guy at the gate, who let him in. Since then, nothing."

Carol was feeling a raw excitement that surprised her. Keeping her voice calm, she said, "Okay, stay here. We'll contact you if we need you."

For a moment, she considered calling Leota, telling her what was happening. But this wasn't her jurisdiction, her area of expertise.

Carol loosened the Glock in the holster in the small of her back, reassured by its sleek deadliness. Bourke was armed with a heavier Smith & Wesson nine millimeter. They didn't say anything to each other, walking down the street side by side in the moonlight, until Bourke laughed softly, and said, "Sort of like *High Noon*, but in the middle of the night."

Carol was prepared to lean on whoever was guarding the gate—arrest him if necessary, so she was pleased to find it was Dave Ledmark.

"Not on bodyguard duty tonight?" said Bourke as he opened the gates for them.

Ledmark jerked his thumb over his shoulder. "Inman's in there. I phoned down, and they said to let him in." He grinned. "And I wasn't to tell anyone Inman was here. Makes you wonder, doesn't it? I had no idea he knew Juanita Paz."

"He didn't ask for Hector?" Carol inquired.

Ledmark shook his head. "Juanita all the way."

"Don't announce us," said Carol. "I'd like it to be a surprise."

They walked down the drive together. Carol had changed into sneakers she kept in the car, so she could move almost silently. It was a beautiful night, cool but still. Dark shadows alternated with silver moonlight. Carol felt as though she were in some alternative black-and-white world.

They stopped to confer just before they reached the house. "Of course we have no search warrant," said Carol, "but we have every reason, do we not, to think a crime is in progress?"

"Every reason."

With shocking abruptness, floodlights sprang to life, illuminating the entire façade of the house and bathing them in a brilliant glare. At the same time a voice behind them said, "Keep your hands where I can see them."

Carol swung around. The heavy automatic was quite steady in his hand. Full of bitter anger with herself to have walked so obligingly into this trap, she said, "Mr. Ledmark, this is a surprise."

"I'm sure it is. Don't move one muscle, either of you."

Hector Paz came running out of the house, a double-barreled shotgun in his hands. "Up! Up!" he shouted, his voice trembling with either fear or excitement. He seemed almost frantic. Faced with his panicky commands, they obediently raised their hands.

"This is ridiculous," said Carol in a calm, reasonable tone. "We're police officers. It's known we're here."

Paz halted, then approached them as if they might bite. Ledmark, a smirk on his face, moved to watch them more closely as Paz, hands

147

shaking, fumbled to take Bourke's gun from his shoulder holster.

Carol would have taken the opportunity to snatch her Glock, had not Ledmark jabbed the barrel of his black automatic into the side of Bourke's neck, saying as he did, "Don't think of it. Move, and he dies." To Paz he said, "Get their phones."

They were marched into the house and through the long corridors, hands linked behind their necks. Carol was alert for any chance to escape, but Paz, breathing heavily as if he'd run a marathon, was behind them with the shotgun trained on their backs. He was so hyped up, Carol feared he might discharge the gun accidentally. Dave Ledmark, quietly efficient, brought up the rear.

In contrast to her brother, Juanita was ice. She looked them over with chilly disdain when they were pushed into the Pazs' room with its stylish contemporary furniture. It was stunning to see the difference in the woman. Gone was the hesitant deference. In its place was implacable determination.

Carol, following training for such hostage situations, attempted to communicate at a conversational level. "Juanita, do you mind if we put our hands down?"

Ignoring this request entirely, Juanita said to Ledmark, "Go back to the gate. Don't let anyone in."

"Look, this is a lot more than I signed on for—"

"You'll be very well paid. Let's say double what we agreed."

This offer clearly pleased Ledmark. "Double? All right." Disconcertingly, he gave Carol a sympathetic look before he left the room. "Sorry this had to happen."

Juanita waited until Ledmark had gone, then said to Hector, "Is Humphries in the boat?"

He nodded, plainly anxious to please. The reversal of roles was quite fascinating, and Carol felt a deep chagrin that she had been fooled. Hector had appeared the one in control, Juanita the timid wife. Carol said to Juanita, "It was you who cut Jim Flint's throat."

She might not have spoken. Juanita said to her husband, "Humphries is alive? Now we have these two"—her gaze flickered over them dispassionately—"it won't do to have him die before they do."

148

"I gave him the injection, as you told me to. He's unconscious."
Bourke said, "So the set-up is that Humphries is to kill us?"

Only Carol, who knew him so well, could detect the slight tremor in his voice. She was feeling what Bourke must be experiencing too—a total disbelief that this was happening, together with burning anger, and paralyzing fear that her life was shortly to be over.

"Where's Chuck Inman?" Carol asked.

"Right here," came from the doorway. Inman tried for a jaunty walk into the room, and failed. His face was haggard and his shoulders stooped, although he kept his hands in the pockets of his shabby jacket in an almost pathetic attempt to be nonchalant.

The first sign of emotion showed on Juanita Paz's face. "You stupid creature," she snapped, "coming here like a frightened dog with its tail between its legs."

He winced, but made an effort to stand up to her. "Look, Juanita, without me you have nothing. *I'm* the one who inherits, *I'm* the one who has the money. Not you."

"That money won't be any comfort, if you're in jail." A small smile touched her lips. "You've only killed secondhand, Chuck. This time you can pull the trigger yourself."

He took a step back. "I can't . . ."

Juanita's lip twisted in a sneer. "Hector has more guts than you." This obviously was not a flattering comparison. Hector flushed red. Inman went to protest, but snapped his jaw shut when Juanita turned her basilisk gaze on him.

The subservient, anxious Juanita had become a detached, frosty commander, who had, at least at the moment, complete control. She put out her hand to her brother, snapped her fingers. He kept the shotgun trained on them as he fumbled in his pocket and took out Carol's Glock. Juanita took it from him and handed it to Inman. "Do you know how to fire this?"

"Jesus, of course I do." With a weak smile, he added, "It doesn't take a rocket scientist to pull a trigger."

Carol visualized the estate. One entire side was taken up by a harbor water frontage. While the surveillance detail waited on the street, it appeared she and Bourke would be marched to a boat, and taken with Humphries out onto the water. There were a myriad destinations within Port Jackson itself, and more if one ventured outside the massive sandstone headlands into the heaving waves of the Pacific Ocean.

"Was Humphries always the fall guy?" she asked. To flatter Juanita, she added, "If so, it was working. We were about to arrest him."

Flattery worked. "It was well done, wasn't it?" said Juanita, her teeth flashing in a quick smile.

Hector, standing beside her, looked gratified. "It was like a military campaign," he said.

"So much planning," said Carol in tones of admiration, "and incredible timing."

Juanita nodded. "You have no idea."

"Of course you had help. Ambrose Slessor, for example. He speaks so highly of you, Juanita."

She narrowed her eyes. "That greedy little man? He's paid well for what he does."

"And what would that be?" Bourke inquired.

Inman, clearly anxious to be included, said, "Slessor's in the dark as to what's going on, but he'll do anything for Juanita."

Inman's declaration tightened Juanita's mouth. "You stupid pig, shut up," she said. "You've always talked too much."

"Now, look—"

"Take these two down to the boat with Hector. You know what to do."

Inman swallowed. "I don't know if I can . . ."

Juanita jerked her head in Bourke and Carol's direction. "Do you think you'll get one cent of your money, if they live? You decide. Be rich for life, or rot in jail."

He let his breath out in a long sigh. "Okay."

Carol caught Bourke's eye, and he gave an almost imperceptible nod. She knew he had evaluated the situation as she had: Juanita was

150

apparently unarmed. Hector had the shotgun trained on them and Bourke's gun in his pocket. Inman had Carol's Glock clutched in one hand.

She and Bourke had to act in the next few minutes, or lose all chance to live. It was clear there was some scenario being set up where Humphries would apparently murder them. Carol glanced at their captors. Juanita remained cool. Hector had calmed down, but was still edgy and tense. Inman looked physically ill.

"We're wasting time," said Juanita. "Get it over and done with now."

Carol nodded to Bourke. They moved simultaneously, Bourke to neutralize Hector, Carol to deal with Juanita and Chuck Inman. For a big man, Bourke moved with blinding speed, slapping the barrels of the shotgun aside with a sweep of his forearm as he chopped at Hector's neck with the edge of his other hand. The blast as one barrel discharged was shockingly loud in the enclosed space.

Inman's mouth opened in a silent shriek as Carol struck at him. He tried to scramble away, but she was upon him. He dropped the Glock, fell to his knees, blood spurting between his fingers as he cupped his broken nose.

She scrabbled for the gun, grabbed it, whirled around. One glance took in the situation: Bourke and Hector were locked in combat, rolling on the floor. Juanita had snatched up the shotgun, and was swinging it around in Carol's direction.

Carol fired. Juanita continued to bring the shotgun to bear. Carol fired again. Juanita's smooth movement stuttered. She and Carol locked eyes. The shotgun wavered, dipped. Juanita looked down to where blood was blossoming on her breast. She took one step back, another. Then, with strange grace, her legs folded and she fell.

Carol leapt to seize the shotgun. With difficulty, Bourke got to his feet. Panting, he looked down at the semi-conscious Hector Paz.

"Carol," he said between gasps, "I've got to get to the gym. I'm just so out of condition."

151

CHAPTER THIRTEEN

Within an hour the Rule estate was the center of both law enforcement and media attention. Helicopters chattered overhead, media vans crammed the surrounding streets, enterprising journalists hired boats and tried to enter by the grounds from the water.

In critical condition, Juanita Paz had been rushed to hospital, a police guard by her side. Still unconscious, Kent Humphries had been similarly transported. Chuck Inman, moaning with the pain of his broken nose, had been driven by two officers to the nearest outpatient clinic for medical attention before being formally charged. David Ledmark had made a run for it, but had been apprehended trying to break into a car several streets away from the estate.

Superintendent Edgar had arrived early to the scene, having his driver pause at the entry gates to ensure the television cameras got a clear shot of his profile. Together with Carol and Bourke, he had returned to the Police Center for the interrogation of Hector Paz, who had been pronounced fit to question by the police doctor.

To Carol's silent fury, Edgar had clearly been about to personally conduct the interrogation, when a call from the Commissioner had instructed him to leave it to the officer in charge. "I'll be monitoring the proceedings from the other side of the one-way mirror, Carol," he said, obviously miffed at his exclusion from the center of the action.

Carol decided to do the interview alone. To establish trust, she began by calling Hector by his first name. The interview began at three o'clock in the morning. She asked him if he were tired, but he shook his head. Carol imagined the events of the evening had given him the same buzz of adrenaline that she had.

Hector Paz was in a curious mood. He seemed to Carol oddly elated for someone about to be interrogated about a series of murders. He'd asked about his wife—"Will she live?" Carol had pointed out Juanita was his sister. He'd nodded agreement, then took the information she was in critical condition quite serenely. Carol wondered if in some sense he was relieved Juanita no longer held authority over him.

Hector had legal representation—a mousy little man with a tight mouth—but proceeded to tell the man he didn't want to be interrupted by legal objections while he answered questions.

Carol had seen this desire to unburden oneself in individuals before, but Hector Paz was an extreme example. He answered every question in full, sometimes in extraordinary detail.

Juanita and he had come up with several possible schemes when they learned Rule had fatal cancer. Before this point, they intended to swindle Rule the way they'd swindled their employer in Colombia, but the opportunities presented by Rule's impending death changed their minds.

"The plan we ultimately decided on evolved through many discussions," Hector said with obvious pride. "We tried out scenario after scenario until we were satisfied." He half-smiled. "I think that was the best part of all. It was like a fascinating game."

They asked themselves who the next heirs would be if Martina died before her father. "Ambrose Slessor helped us, and didn't ask too many questions. He's infatuated with Juanita, and even then he was stealing from Rule."

Rosalie Webb would be the principal heir, and she was clearly not corruptible, so she would have to be eliminated. With her gone, the field for inheritance of the huge fortune expanded—ten people, including Rosalie's son and daughter. Fred Verrell, who'd been recommended by Slessor, carried out background checks. Chuck Inman turned out to be a perfect candidate to join the conspiracy, being a con artist who was both greedy and over-confident.

That plan was put on hold when Martina made a will in favor of Juanita. The idea immediately became to wait until Rule died and Martina inherited his billions. Then she'd almost immediately be killed in an accident, and Juanita would have it all. However, when Martina cooled on the friendship, accusing Juanita—quite accurately—of manipulating her for what she could get, and changed her will, they reverted to the original scheme.

"You set up a fall guy, to eventually take the blame for the murders," Carol observed.

Kent Humphries had proved an ideal candidate for the role. Reclusive, except for the rugby club he belonged to, Kent Humphries had no close friends. He made few phone calls. And as a bonus, he had pathological distrust of lawyers that could be exploited. A flight attendant, it was easy to trace his pattern of work. The Bondi apartment would be bugged, and one of Verrell's most trusted operatives would keep watch to make sure Humphries was alone at the time of each murder.

"Do you know the name of the person Verrell used?"

"I know every detail," Hector Paz declared, almost smug. "Rob

154

Wells. He does anything Verrell wants, legal or illegal. We used him to make the first approach to Chuck Inman."

Inman had eagerly come to Australia. Secret meetings to explain the scheme cemented the deal. When he left the country, the Webbs were killed.

"The Webb accident was like a practice run," said Hector. "I'd done a lot of sailing in Colombia, and knew exactly what to do." He'd driven to South Australia, rigged the boat, and waited for the explosion. Ricky Webb had survived. He was to be dealt with later.

Carol took him through the murders, one by one, chilled by his obvious pride in the manner in which each had been accomplished.

Using Verrell's contacts, two lowlifes who belonged to Humphries' football club and who would do anything for the right amount, were hired to carry out the faked accident. They were well paid, but didn't enjoy the money for long. Hector took Doherty for a one-way ride, dumping his weighted body in a reservoir. Hawkins unexpectedly took off for Bali. A local hoodlum was paid to kill him in a staged brawl.

An overdose of morphine disposed of Thurmond Rule.

"What about Fancee Porter in the States?" Carol asked.

"It was a real accident. She was going to be eliminated later, when Inman wasn't in the country. Inman set it up for Humphries to meet her, so there'd be evidence of a contact between them. It was a stroke of luck when she died."

Hector looked gratified when Carol mentioned Ian Stewart. "That worked so well. I knocked at the door wearing a gas company uniform and said a leak had been reported in the area. Struck up a conversation about chess. He offered me coffee. I put a solution of Valium in his mug. Juanita came in when he was asleep, typed the suicide note, and helped me arrange him on the bed."

"This was a staged suicide, but Flint's death was obviously a murder."

"We didn't want to be obvious to begin with, because Humphries would be arrested too soon, but we couldn't wait too long either, because something might go wrong."

Jim Flint's death had been the first overt murder, and Juanita had decided it had to be shocking, in order to get attention. Wells confirmed Kent Humphries was alone before Juanita met with Flint in the parking area of the pub.

"Juanita told him she knew somewhere very private where they could have sex. I was already there, parked out of sight. Juanita cut Flint's throat herself—I couldn't do it. I was waiting with plastic booties for her feet and a coat to put on to soak up the blood. We didn't leave any clues, did we?"

"It was well done."

Hector half-smiled. "I remember Juanita was very pleased."

"And last night, your wife killed Nicholas Jordan."

"That's right. She was in a nurse's uniform. Blended in with the rest of the staff."

The whole interview was being recorded, and would be transcribed in full, but Carol had made her own notes as well.

"Have I got this right? Juanita's in charge of the whole conspiracy?"

As the interview had progressed, Hector had been enthusiastic. Now he seemed to deflate a little. "We worked as partners."

"Who had the final say?"

He gave a slight shrug. "Juanita, I suppose."

"She murdered three people by her own hand—Thurmond Rule, Jim Flint and Nicholas Jordan?"

"And she helped with Stewart," he reminded her.

"You, yourself, have killed three members of the Webb family, plus Sid Doherty and Ian Stewart."

"That's right."

"At this point, Chuck Inman hadn't killed anybody, yet he was going to inherit all the money."

"We had his guarantee in writing of the millions he'd invest in companies we'd set up. Juanita knew he was a loudmouthed fool, who'd try to swindle us once he had the money, so we recorded every meeting with him on video. And she was going to make sure

156

he had blood on his hands. It was going to be Dave Ledmark, but then you came along."

"Chuck Inman told some stupid lies," said Carol.

Hector made an exasperated sound. "Juanita was so angry with him when he lied to you about visiting Australia. She told him it was an unnecessary risk, but Inman didn't care. He was having so much fun with all the attention he was getting."

"How many more murders did you have planned?"

"Ricky Webb was to die in an accident—something like his bicycle being hit by a car. Juanita didn't want to kill Ophelia Rule—she said Humphries would be arrested soon, and after that it was too dangerous to kill off another heir if he couldn't be blamed."

Carol asked a question that had puzzled her. "Why were the family trees sent anonymously? What was the point?"

"For our scheme to work, we needed all the heirs to come forward. Ophelia Rule was sent one because she'd make a fuss and create publicity. And Stewart was the type who probably wouldn't realize he could claim an inheritance. Of course, we soon found nobody needed encouragement. The scent of money was enough."

Carol stopped the interview for a bathroom break and to get a supply of fresh coffee. When she resumed, she said, "How did Humphries end up at the estate last night?"

Hector was beginning to look tired. He rubbed his face, yawned, and said, "Rob Wells was watching him while Juanita killed Jordan. He'd made sure Humphries' phone wasn't working, so there's no way a call could give him an alibi. Wells had orders to stop him if he left his apartment. Just at the wrong time, Humphries came out and started walking in the direction of the club. Wells offered him a lift, knocked him out, and called me."

Carol was fascinated to see Hector Paz was embarrassed. "I made a big mistake," he said. "I told Wells to bring Humphries to the estate. Juanita was furious when she came home. Wells had gone and Humphries was coming to, so she told me to give him an injection. I'd just done it when Ledmark called and said you were on

157

your way down to the house. That only gave as a few minutes to work out what to do." He sounded aggrieved at Carol and Bourke's lack of consideration.

Hector explained Rule's boat was kept fueled and ready to go as an escape route in case it was ever needed. "The best we could think off was to make it look like you'd tried to arrest Humphries and he'd fired and killed you both, but one of you had shot him too, so he dies on the boat trying to get away."

"Where does David Ledmark fit in?"

"He didn't have anything to do with it until a few days ago. He's a bodyguard for Inman, and you already know how Inman talks too much. Ledmark got suspicious and started asking questions. Juanita offered him a quarter of a million dollars after the will is settled, and he took it with both hands."

Carol stood, stretched. "Thank you, Hector. I'll let you get some rest. There'll be more questions later."

Outside the room Bourke was waiting for her. She looked around. "Where's Edgar?"

"Gone home to get ready to shine in the breakfast media," said Bourke with heavy sarcasm. "But let me give you the good news, Carol. Ambrose Slessor? Accomplice to murder, before and after the fact. There are sure to be embezzlement charges to follow. Fred Verrell and Rob Wells? The same murder charges. Haven't decided on the charges for Ledmark yet, but he won't be happy. Right now he's being held for breaking into a car."

He patted her shoulder. "You should go home."

"I'm on my way. How's Kent Humphries?"

"Fine. He's regained consciousness."

"And Juanita Paz?"

"She died twenty minutes ago."

• • •

Last night Carol had called Leota at the first opportunity to tell her she wouldn't be home until some time the next day. "It's

158

Saturday, honey. I'll be here."

Aunt Sarah had gone back to the mountains in the Eco-Crone bus, so Carol and Leota would be alone. Carol drove with great care, squinting through her dark glasses at the glare of morning sunshine. She was so tired she felt disconnected from her body.

She negotiated the familiar streets near her home with frowning concentration. Pulling into the carport, she sat, unwilling to move, looking through the windscreen at a flock of screeching white cockatoos, who were good-naturedly bullying each other in the top branches of her tallest eucalyptus gum tree.

"My tree," she said.

It took concentration to drag herself out of the car, unlatch the gate, and walk down the path to the front door. She heard herself saying, idiotically, "My gate, my path, my front door."

Leota folded her into a warm hug. "You must be exhausted. I'll make you breakfast, then put you to bed."

Unresisting, Carol allowed herself to be led into the kitchen. She perched on a stool, watching as if from a great distance, as Leota expertly made an omelet.

"Leota?"

"Yes?"

"I can't come to America."

Leota put down the spatula. "You mean right now, or do you mean not ever?"

She could slide off the stool and curl up on the floor and be asleep in an instant. "I mean I can't come to America. That's all I can say."

"We'll talk about it later, okay?"

She thought, *It won't do any good*, but didn't say it.

Twenty minutes later she was in bed, sliding into a blessed sleep that rushed to meet her. Her last conscious thought curved her lips in a smile: *Chief Inspector Carol Ashton.*

MAYBE NEXT TIME by Karin Kallmaker. 256 pp. Sabrina
Starling always believed in maybe next time . . . until now.
ISBN 1-931513-26-0 $12.95

WHEN GOOD GIRLS GO BAD: A Motor City Thriller by
Therese Szymanski. 230 pp. Brett, Randi, and Allie join forces
to stop a serial killer.   ISBN 1-931513-11-2   12.95

A DAY TOO LONG: A Helen Black Mystery by Pat Welch.
328 pp. This time Helen's fate is in her own hands.
ISBN 1-931513-22-8 $12.95

THE RED LINE OF YARMALD by Diana Rivers. 256 pp.
The Hadra's only hope lies in a magical red line . . . Climactic
sequel to *Clouds of War.*   ISBN 1-931513-23-6 $12.95

OUTSIDE THE FLOCK by Jackie Calhoun. 224 pp.
Jo embraces her new love and life.   ISBN 1-931513-13-9 $12.95

LEGACY OF LOVE by Marianne K. Martin. 224 pp. Read the whole
Sage Bristo story.   ISBN 1-931513-15-5 $12.95

STREET RULES: A Detective Franco Mystery by Baxter Clare.
304 pp. Gritty, fast-paced mystery with compelling Detective
L.A. Franco   ISBN 1-931513-14-7 $12.95

RECOGNITION FACTOR: 4th Denise Cleever Thriller by
Claire McNab. 176 pp. Denise Cleever tracks a notorious
terrorist to America.   ISBN 1-931513-24-4 $12.95

NORA AND LIZ by Nancy Garden. 296 pp. Lesbian romance
by the author of *Annie on My Mind.*   ISBN 1931513-20-1 $12.95

MIDAS TOUCH by Frankie J. Jones. 208 pp. Sandra had
everything but love.   ISBN 1-931513-21-X $12.95

BEYOND ALL REASON by Peggy J. Herring. 240 pp. A
romance hotter than Texas.   ISBN 1-9513-25-2 $12.95

ACCIDENTAL MURDER: 14th Detective Inspector Carol
Ashton Mystery by Claire McNab. 208 pp.Carol Ashton
tracks an elusive killer.   ISBN 1-931513-16-3 $12.95

SEEDS OF FIRE:Tunnel of Light Trilogy, Book 2 by Karin
Kallmaker writing as Laura Adams. 274 pp. Intriguing sequel to
Sleight of Hand.   ISBN 1-931513-19-8 $12.95

DRIFTING AT THE BOTTOM OF THE WORLD by
Auden Bailey. 288 pp. Beautifully written first novel set in
Antarctica.   ISBN 1-931513-17-1 $12.95

CLOUDS OF WAR by Diana Rivers. 288 pp. Women unite
to defend Zelindar!   ISBN 1-931513-12-0 $12.95

DEATHS OF JOCASTA: 2nd Micky Knight Mystery by J.M.
Redmann. 408 pp. Sexy and intriguing Lambda Literary Award-
nominated mystery.   ISBN 1-931513-10-4 $12.95

LOVE IN THE BALANCE by Marianne K. Martin. 256 pp.
The classic lesbian love story, back in print! ISBN 1-931513-08-2 $12.95

THE COMFORT OF STRANGERS by Peggy J. Herring. 272 pp.
Lela's work was her passion . . . until now. ISBN 1-931513-09-0 $12.95

CHICKEN by Paula Martinac. 208 pp. Lynn finds that the
only thing harder than being in a lesbian relationship is ending
one.   ISBN 1-931513-07-4 $11.95

TAMARACK CREEK by Jackie Calhoun. 208 pp. An intriguing
story of love and danger.   ISBN 1-931513-06-6 $11.95

DEATH BY THE RIVERSIDE: 1st Micky Knight Mystery by
J.M. Redmann. 320 pp. Finally back in print, the book that
launched the Lambda Literary Award-winning Micky Knight
mystery series.   ISBN 1-931513-05-8 $11.95

EIGHTH DAY: A Cassidy James Mystery by Kate Calloway.
272 pp. In the eighth installment of the Cassidy James
mystery series, Cassidy goes undercover at a camp for troubled
teens.   ISBN 1-931513-04-X $11.95

MIRRORS by Marianne K. Martin. 208 pp. Jean Carson and Shayna
Bradley fight for a future together.   ISBN 1-931513-02-3 $11.95

THE ULTIMATE EXIT STRATEGY: A Virginia Kelly
Mystery by Nikki Baker. 240 pp. The long-awaited return of
the wickedly observant Virginia Kelly.   ISBN 1-931513-03-1 $11.95

FOREVER AND THE NIGHT by Laura DeHart Young. 224 pp.
Desire and passion ignite the frozen Arctic in this exciting
sequel to the classic romantic adventure *Love on the Line*.
ISBN 0-931513-00-7 $11.95

WINGED ISIS by Jean Stewart. 240 pp. The long-awaited
sequel to *Warriors of Isis* and the fourth in the exciting Isis
series. ISBN 1-931513-01-5 $11.95

ROOM FOR LOVE by Frankie J. Jones. 192 pp. Jo and Beth
must overcome the past in order to have a future together.
ISBN 0-9677753-9-6 $11.95

THE QUESTION OF SABOTAGE by Bonnie J. Morris.
144 pp. A charming, sexy tale of romance, intrigue, and
coming of age. ISBN 0-9677753-8-8 $11.95

SLEIGHT OF HAND by Karin Kallmaker writing as
Laura Adams. 256 pp. A journey of passion, heartbreak
and triumph that reunites two women for a final chance at
their destiny. ISBN 0-9677753-7-X $11.95

MOVING TARGETS: A Helen Black Mystery by Pat Welch.
240 pp. Helen must decide if getting to the bottom of a mystery
is worth hitting bottom. ISBN 0-9677753-6-1 $11.95

CALM BEFORE THE STORM by Peggy J. Herring. 208 pp.
Colonel Robicheaux retires from the military and comes out of
the closet. ISBN 0-9677753-1-0 $12.95

OFF SEASON by Jackie Calhoun. 208 pp. Pam threatens Jenny
and Rita's fledgling relationship. ISBN 0-9677753-0-2 $11.95

WHEN EVIL CHANGES FACE: A Motor City Thriller by
Therese Szymanski. 240 pp. Brett Higgins is back in another
heart-pounding thriller. ISBN 0-9677753-3-7 $11.95

BOLD COAST LOVE by Diana Tremain Braund. 208 pp.
Jackie Claymont fights for her reputation and the right to love
the woman she chooses. ISBN 0-9677753-2-9 $11.95

THE WILD ONE by Lyn Denison. 176 pp. Rachel never
expected that Quinn's wild yearnings would change her life
forever. ISBN 0-9677753-4-5 $12.95

SWEET FIRE by Saxon Bennett. 224 pp. Welcome to
Heroy—the town with the most lesbians per capita than any
other place on the planet! ISBN 0-9677753-5-3 $11.95